The Story of the Pony Express

Glenn D. Bradley

Contents

THE STORY OF THE PONY EXPRESS

BY

Glenn D. Bradley

To My Parents

Preface

This little volume has but one purpose - to give an authentic, useful, and readable account of the Pony Express. This wonderful enterprise played an important part in history, and demonstrated what American spirit can accomplish. It showed that the "heroes of sixty-one" were not all south of Mason and Dixon's line fighting each other. And, strange to say, little of a formal nature has been written concerning it.

I have sought to bring to light and make accessible to all readers the more important facts of the Pony Express - its inception, organization and development, its importance to history, its historical background, and some of the anecdotes incidental to its operation. The subject leads one into a wide range of fascinating material, all interesting though much of it is irrelevant. In itself this material is fragmentary and incoherent. It would be quite easy to fill many pages with western adventure having no special bearing upon the central topic. While I have diverged occasionally from the thread of the narrative, my purpose has been merely to give where possible more background to the story, that the account as a whole might be more understandable in its relation to the general facts of history.

Special acknowledgment is due Frank A. Root of Topeka, Kansas, joint author with William E. Connelley of The Overland Stage To California, an excellent compendium of data on many phases of the subject. In preparing this work, various Senate Documents have been of great value. Some interesting material is found in Inman and Cody's Salt Lake Trail.

The files of the Century Magazine, old newspaper files, Bancroft's colossal history of the West and the works of Samuel L. Clemens have also been of value in compiling the present book.

G.D.B.

Chapter I
At A Nation's Crisis

The Pony Express was the first rapid transit and the first fast mail line across the continent from the Missouri River to the Pacific Coast. It was a system by means of which messages were carried swiftly on horseback across the plains and deserts, and over the mountains of the far West. It brought the Atlantic coast and the Pacific slope ten days nearer to each other.

It had a brief existence of only sixteen months and was supplanted by the transcontinental telegraph. Yet it was of the greatest importance in binding the East and West together at a time when overland travel was slow and cumbersome, and when a great national crisis made the rapid communication of news between these sections an imperative necessity.

The Pony Express marked the highest development in overland travel prior to the coming of the Pacific railroad, which it preceded nine years. It, in fact, proved the feasibility of a transcontinental road and demonstrated that such a line could be built and operated continuously the year around - a feat that had always been regarded as impossible.

The operation of the Pony Express was a supreme achievement of physical endurance on the part of man and his ever faithful companion, the horse. The history of this organization should be a lasting monument to the physical sacrifice of man and beast in an effort to accomplish something worth while. Its history should be an enduring tribute to American courage and American organizing genius.

The fall of Fort Sumter in April, 1861, did not produce the Civil War crisis. For many months, the gigantic struggle then imminent, had been painfully discernible to far-seeing men. In 1858, Lincoln had forewarned the country in his "House Divided" speech. As early as the beginning of the year 1860 the Union had been plainly in jeopardy. Early in February of that momentous year, Jefferson Davis, on behalf of the South, had introduced his famous resolutions in the Senate of the United States. This document was the ultimatum of the dissatisfied slave-holding commonwealths. It demanded that Congress should protect slavery throughout the domain of the United States. The territories, it declared, were the common property of the states of the Union and hence open to the citizens of all states with all their personal possessions. The Northern states, furthermore, were no longer to interfere with the working of the Fugitive Slave Act. They must repeal their Personal Liberty laws and respect the Dred Scott Decision of the Federal Supreme Court. Neither in their own legislatures nor in Congress should they trespass upon the right of the South to regulate slavery as it best saw fit.

These resolutions, demanding in effect that slavery be thus safeguarded - almost to the extent of introducing it into the free states - really foreshadowed the Democratic platform of 1860 which led to the great split in that party, the victory of the Republicans under Lincoln, the subsequent secession of the more radical southern states, and finally the Civil War, for it was inevitable that the North, when once aroused, would bitterly resent such pro-slavery demands.

And this great crisis was only the bursting into flame of many smaller fires that had long been smoldering. For generations the two sections had been drifting apart. Since the middle of the seventeenth century, Mason and Dixon's line had been a line of real division separating two inherently distinct portions of the country.

By 1860, then, war was inevitable. Naturally, the conflict would at once present intricate military problems, and among them the retention of the Pacific Coast was of the deepest concern to the Union. Situated at a distance of nearly two thousand miles from the Missouri river which was then the nation's western frontier, this intervening space comprised trackless plains, almost impenetrable ranges of snow-capped mountains, and parched alkali deserts. And besides these barriers of nature which lay between the West coast and the settled eastern half of the country, there were many fierce tribes of savages who were usually on the alert to oppose the movements of the white race through their dominions.

California, even then, was the jewel of the Pacific. Having a considerable population, great natural wealth, and unsurpassed climate and fertility, she was jealously desired by both the North and the South.

To the South, the acquisition of California meant enhanced prestige - involving, as it would, the occupation of a large area whose soils and climate might encourage the perpetuation of slavery; it meant a rich possession which would afford her a strategic base for waging war against her northern foe; it meant a romantic field in which opportunity might be given to organize an allied republic of the Pacific, a power which would, perchance, forcibly absorb the entire Southwest and a large section of Northern Mexico. By thus creating counter forces the South would effectively block the Federal Government on the western half of the continent.

The North also desired the prestige that would come from holding California as well as the material strength inherent in the state's valuable resources. Moreover to hold this region would give the North a base of operations to check her opponent in any campaign of aggression in the far West, should the South presume such an attempt. And the possession of California would also offer to the North the very best means of protecting the Western frontier, one of the Union's most vulnerable points of attack.

It was with such vital conditions that the Pony Express was identified; it was in retaining California for the Union, and in helping incidentally to preserve the Union, that the Express became an important factor in American history.

Not to mention the romance, the unsurpassed courage, the unflinching endurance, and the wonderful exploits which the routine operations of the Pony Express involved, its identity with problems of nation-wide and world-wide importance make its story seem worth telling. And with its romantic existence and its place in history the succeeding pages of this book will briefly deal.

Chapter II
Inception and Organization of the Pony Express

Following the discovery of gold in California in January 1848, that region sprang into immediate prominence. From all parts of the country and the remote corners of the earth came the famous Forty-niners. Amid the chaos of a great mining camp the Anglo-Saxon love of law and order soon asserted itself. Civil and religious institutions quickly arose, and, in the summer of 1850, a little more than a year after the big rush had started, California entered the Union as a free state.

The boom went on and the census of 1860 revealed a population of 380,000 in the new commonwealth. And when to these figures were added those of Oregon and Washington Territory, an aggregate of 444,000 citizens of the United States were found to be living on the Pacific Slope. Crossing the Sierras eastward and into the Great Basin, 47,000 more were located in the Territories of Nevada and Utah, - thus making a grand total of nearly a half million people beyond the Rocky Mountains in 1860. And these figures did not include Indians nor Chinese.

Without reference to any military phase of the problem, this detached population obviously demanded and deserved adequate mail and transportation facilities. How to secure the quickest and most dependable communication with the populous sections of the East had long been a serious proposition. Private corporations and Congress had not been wholly insensible to the needs of the West. Subsidized stage routes had for some years been in operation, and by the close of 1858 several lines were well-equipped and doing much business over the so-called Southern and Central routes. Perhaps the most common route for sending mail from the East to the Pacific Coast was by steamship from New York to Panama where it was unloaded, hurried across the Isthmus, and again shipped by water to San Francisco. All these lines of traffic were slow and tedious, a letter in any case requiring from three to four weeks to reach its destination. The need of a more rapid system of communication between the East and West at once became apparent and it was to supply this need that the Pony Express really came into existence.

The story goes that in the autumn of 1854, United States Senator William Gwin of California was making an overland trip on horseback from San Francisco to Washington, D. C. He was following the Central route via Salt Lake and South Pass, and during a portion of his journey he had for a traveling companion, Mr. B. F. Ficklin, then General Superintendent for the big freighting and stage firm of Russell, Majors, and Waddell of Leavenworth. Ficklin, it seems, was a resourceful and progressive man, and had long been engaged in the overland transportation business. He had already conceived an idea for establishing a much closer transit service between the Missouri river and the Coast, but, as is the case with many innovators, had never gained a serious hearing. He had the traffic agent's natural desire to better the existing service in the territory which his line served; and he had the ambition of a loyal employee to put into effect a plan that would bring added honor and preferment to his firm. In addition to possessing these worthy ideals, it is perhaps not unfair to state that Ficklin was personally ambitious.

Nevertheless, Ficklin confided his scheme enthusiastically to Senator Gwin, at the same time pointing out the benefits that would accrue to California should it ever be put into execution. The Senator at once saw the merits of the plan and quickly caught the contagion. Not only was he enough of a statesman to appreciate the worth of a fast mail line across the continent, but he was also a good enough politician to realize that his position with his constituents and the country at large might be greatly strengthened were he to champion the enactment of a popular measure that would encourage the building of such a line through the aid of a Federal subsidy.

So in January, 1855, Gwin introduced in the Senate a bill which proposed to establish a weekly letter express service between St. Louis and San Francisco. The express was to operate on a ten-day schedule, follow the Central Route, and was to receive a compensation not exceeding $500.00 for each round trip. This bill was referred to the Committee on Military Affairs where it was quietly tabled and "killed."

For the next five years the attention of Congress was largely taken up with the anti-slavery troubles that led to secession and war. Although the people of the West, and the Pacific Coast in particular, continued to agitate the need of a new and quick through mail service, for a long time little was done. It has been claimed that southern representatives in Congress during the decade before the war managed to prevent any legislation favorable to overland mail routes running North of the slave-holding states; and that they concentrated their strength to render government aid to the southern routes whenever possible.

At that time there were three generally recognized lines of mail traffic, of which the Panama line was by far the most important. Next came the so-called southern or "Butterfield" route which started from St. Louis and ran far to the southward, entering California from the extreme southeast corner of the state; a goodly amount of mail being sent in this direction. The Central route followed the Platte River into Wyoming and reached Sacramento via Salt Lake City, almost from a due easterly direction. On account of its location this route or trail could be easily controlled by the North in case of war. It had received very meagre support from the Government, and carried as a rule, only local mail. While the most direct route to San Francisco, it had been rendered the least important. This was not due solely to Congressional manipulation. Because of its northern latitude and the numerous high mountain ranges it traversed, this course was often blockaded with deep snows and was generally regarded as extremely difficult of access during the winter months.

While a majority of the people of California were loyal to the Union, there was a vigorous minority intensely in sympathy with the southern cause and ready to conspire for, or bring about by force of arms if necessary, the secession of their state. As the Civil War became more and more imminent, it became obvious to Union men in both East and West that the existing lines of communication were untrustworthy. Just as soon as trouble should start, the Confederacy could, and most certainly would, gain control of the southern mail routes. Once in control, she could isolate the Pacific coast for many months and thus enable her sympathizers there the more effectually to perfect their plans of secession. Or she might take advantage of these lines of travel, and, by striking swiftly and suddenly, organize and reinforce her followers in California, intimidate the Unionists, many of whom were apathetic, and by a single bold stroke snatch the prize away from her antagonist before the latter should have had time to act.

To avert this crisis some daring and original plan of communication had to be organized to keep the East and West in close contact with each other; and the Pony Express was the fulfillment of such a plan, for it made a close cooperation between the California loyalists and the Federal Government possible until after the crisis did pass. Yet, strange as it may seem, this providential enterprise was not brought into existence nor even materially aided by the Government. It was organized and operated by a private corporation after having been encouraged in its inception by a United States Senator who later turned traitor to his country.

It finally happened that in the winter of 1859-60, Mr. William Russell, senior partner of the firm of Russell, Majors, and Waddell, was called to Washington in connection with some Government freight contracts. While there he chanced to become acquainted with Senator Gwin who, having been aroused, as we have seen, several years before, by one of the firm's subordinates, at once brought before Mr. Russell the need of better mail connections over the Central route, and of the especial need of better communication should war occur.

Russell at once awoke to the situation. While a loyal citizen and fully alive to the strategic importance which the matter involved, he also believed that he saw a good business opening. Could his firm but grasp the opportunity, and demonstrate the possibility of keeping the Central route open during the winter months, and could they but lower the schedule of the Panama line, a Government contract giving them a virtual monopoly in carrying the transcontinental mail might eventually be theirs.

He at once hurried West, and at Fort Leavenworth met his partners, Messrs. Majors and Waddell, to whom he confidently submitted the new proposition. Much to Russell's chagrin, these gentlemen were not elated over the plan. While passively interested, they keenly foresaw the great cost which a year around overland fast mail service would involve. They were unable to see any chance of the enterprise paying expenses, to say nothing of profits. But Russell, with cheerful optimism, contended that while the project might temporarily be a losing venture, it would pay out in time. He asserted that the opportunity of making good with a hard undertaking - one that had been held impossible of realization - would be a strong asset to the firm's reputation. He also declared that in his conversation with Gwin he had already committed their company to the undertaking, and he did not see how they could, with honor and propriety, evade the responsibility of attempting it. Knowledge of the last mentioned fact at once enlisted the support or his partners. Probably no firm has ever surpassed in integrity that of Russell, Majors, and Waddell, famous throughout the West in the freighting and mail business before the advent of railroads in that section of the men, the verbal promise of one of their number was a binding guarantee and as sacredly respected as a bonded obligation. Finding themselves thus committed, they at once began preparations with tremendous activity. All this happened early in the year 1860.

The first step was to form a corporation, the more adequately to conduct the enterprise; and to that end the Central Overland California and Pike's Peak Express Company was organized under a charter granted by the Territory of Kansas. Besides the three original members of the firm, the incorporators included General Superintendent B. F. Ficklin, together with F. A. Bee, W. W. Finney, and John S. Jones, all tried and trustworthy stage employees who were retained on account of their wide experience in the overland traffic business. The new concern then took over the old stage line from Atchison to Salt Lake City and purchased the mail route and outfit then operating between Salt Lake City and Sacramento. The latter, which had been running a monthly round trip stage between these terminals, was known as the West End Division of the Central Route, and was called the Chorpenning line.

Besides conducting the Pony Express, the corporation aimed to continue a large passenger and freighting business, so it next absorbed the Leavenworth and Pike's Peak Express Co., which had been organized a year previously and had maintained a daily stage between Leavenworth and Denver, on the Smoky Hill River Route.

By mutual agreement, Mr. Russell assumed managerial charge of the Eastern Division of the Pony Express line which lay between St. Joseph and Salt Lake City. Ficklin was stationed at Salt Lake City, the middle point, in a similar capacity. Finney was made Western manager with headquarters at San Francisco. These men now had to revise the route to be traversed, equip it with relay or relief stations which must be provisioned for men and horses, hire dependable men as station-keepers and riders, and buy high grade horses[1] or ponies for the entire course, nearly two thousand miles in extent. Between St. Joseph and Salt Lake City, the company had its old stage route which was already well supplied with stations. West of Salt Lake the old Chorpenning route had been poorly equipped, which made it necessary to erect new stations over much of this course of more than seven hundred miles. The entire line of travel had to be altered in many places, in some instances to shorten the distance, and in others, to avoid as much as possible, wild places where Indians might easily ambush the riders.

The management was fortunate in having the assistance of expert subordinates. A. B. Miller of Leavenworth, a noteworthy employe of the original firm, was invaluable in helping to formulate the general plans of organization. At Salt Lake City, Ficklin secured the services of J. C. Brumley, resident agent of the company, whose vast knowledge of the route and the country that it covered enabled him quickly to work out a schedule, and to ascertain with remarkable accuracy the number of relay and supply stations, their best location, and also the number of horses and men needed. At Carson City, Nevada, Bolivar Roberts, local superintendent of the Western Division, hired upwards of sixty riders, cool-headed nervy men, hardened by years of life in the open. Horses were purchased throughout the West. They were the best that money could buy and ranged from tough California cayuses or mustangs to thoroughbred stock from Iowa. They were bought at an average figure of $200.00 each, a high price in those days. The men were the pick of the frontier; no more expressive description of their qualities can be given. They were hired at salaries varying from $50.00 to $150.00 per month, the riders receiving the highest pay of any below executive rank. When fully equipped, the line comprised 190 stations, about 420 horses, 400 station men and assistants and eighty riders. These are approximate figures, as they varied slightly from time to time.

Perfecting these plans and assembling this array of splendid equipment had been no easy task, yet so well had the organizers understood their business, and so persistently, yet quietly, had they worked, that they accomplished their purpose and made ready within two months after the project had been launched. The public was scarcely aware of what was going on until conspicuous advertisements announced the Pony Express. It was planned to open the line early in April.

Note:

[1] While always called the Pony Express, there were many blooded horses as well as ponies in the service. The distinction between these types of animals is of

course well known to the average reader. Probably "Pony" Express "sounded better" than any other name for the service, hence the adoption of this name by the firm and the public at large. This book will use the words horse and pony indiscriminately.

Chapter III
The First Trip and Triumph

On March 26, 1860, there appeared simultaneously in the St. Louis Republic and the New York Herald the following notice:

To San Francisco in 8 days by the Central Overland California and Pike's Peak Express Company. The first courier of the Pony Express will leave the Missouri River on Tuesday April 3rd at 5 o'clock P. M. and will run regularly weekly hereafter, carrying a letter mail only. The point of departure on the Missouri River will be in telegraphic connection with the East and will be announced in due time.

Telegraphic messages from all parts of the United States and Canada in connection with the point of departure will be received up to 5 o'clock P. M. of the day of leaving and transmitted over the Placerville and St. Joseph telegraph wire to San Francisco and intermediate points by the connecting express, in 8 days.

The letter mail will be delivered in San Francisco in ten days from the departure of the Express. The Express passes through Forts Kearney, Laramie, Bridger, Great Salt Lake City, Camp Floyd, Carson City, The Washoe Silver Mines, Placerville, and Sacramento.

Letters for Oregon, Washington Territory, British Columbia, the Pacific Mexican ports, Russian Possessions, Sandwich Islands, China, Japan and India will be mailed in San Francisco.

Special messengers, bearers of letters to connect with the express the 3rd of April, will receive communications for the courier of that day at No. 481 Tenth St., Washington City, up to 2:45 P. M. on Friday, March 30, and in New York at the office of J. B. Simpson, Room No. 8, Continental Bank Building, Nassau Street, up to 6:30 A. M. of March 31.

Full particulars can be obtained on application at the above places and from the agents of the Company.

This sudden announcement of the long desired fast mail route aroused great enthusiasm in the West and especially in St. Joseph, Missouri, Salt Lake City, and the cities of California, where preparations to celebrate the opening of the line were at once begun. Slowly the time passed, until the afternoon of the eventful day, April 3rd, that was to mark the first step in annihilating distance between the East and West. A great crowd had assembled on the streets of St. Joseph, Missouri. Flags were flying and a brass band added to the jubilation. The Hannibal and St. Joseph Railroad had arranged to run a special train into the city, bringing the through mail from connecting points in the East. Everybody was anxious and excited. At last the shrill whistle of a locomotive was heard, and the train rumbled in - on time. The pouches were rushed to the post office where the express mail was made ready.

The people now surge about the old "Pike's Peak Livery Stables," just South of Pattee Park. All are hushed with subdued expectancy. As the moment of departure approaches, the doors swing open and a spirited horse is led out. Nearby, closely inspecting the animal's equipment is a wiry little man scarcely twenty years old.

Time to go! Everybody back! A pause of seconds, and a cannon booms in the distance - the starting signal. The rider leaps to his saddle and starts. In less than a minute he is at the post office where the letter pouch, square in shape with four padlocked pockets, is awaiting him. Dismounting only long enough for this pouch to be thrown over his saddle, he again springs to his place and is gone. A short sprint and he has reached the Missouri River wharf. A ferry boat under a full head of steam is waiting. With scarcely checked speed, the horse thunders onto the deck of the craft. A rumbling of machinery, the jangle of a bell, the sharp toot of a whistle and the boat has swung clear and is headed straight for the opposite shore. The crowd behind breaks into tumultuous applause. Some scream themselves hoarse; others are strangely silent; and some - strong men - are moved to tears.

The noise of the cheering multitude grows faint as the Kansas shore draws near. The engines are reversed; a swish of water, and the, craft grates against the dock. Scarcely has the gang plank been lowered than horse and rider dash over it and are off at a furious gallop. Away on the jet black steed goes Johnnie Frey, the first rider, with the mail that must be hurled by flesh and blood over 1,966 miles of desolate space - across the plains, through North-eastern Kansas and into Nebraska, up the valley of the Platte, across the Great Plateau, into the foothills and over the summit of the Rockies, into the arid Great Basin, over the Wahsatch range, into the valley of Great Salt Lake, through the terrible alkali deserts of Nevada, through the parched Sink of the Carson River, over the snowy Sierras, and into the Sacramento Valley - the mail must go without delay. Neither storms, fatigue, darkness, rugged mountains, burning deserts, nor savage Indians were to hinder this pouch of letters. The mail must go; and its schedule, incredible as it seemed, must be made. It was a sublime undertaking, than which few have ever put the fibre of Americans to a severer test.

The managers of the Central Overland, California and Pike's Peak Express Company had laid their plans well. Horses and riders for fresh relays, together with station agents and helpers, were ready and waiting at the appointed places, ten or fifteen miles apart over the entire course. There was no guess-work or delay.

After crossing the Missouri River, out of St. Joseph, the official route[2] of the west-bound Pony Express ran at first west and south through Kansas to Kennekuk; then northwest, across the Kickapoo Indian reservation, to Granada, Log Chain, Seneca, Ash Point, Guittards, Marysville, and Hollenberg. Here the valley of the Little Blue River was followed, still in a northwest direction. The trail crossed into Nebraska near Rock Creek and pushed on through Big Sandy and Liberty Farm, to Thirty-two-mile Creek. From thence it passed over the prairie divide to the Platte River, the valley of which was followed to Fort Kearney. This route had already been made famous by the Mormons when they journeyed to Utah in 1847. It had also been followed by many of the California gold-seekers in 1848-49 and by Gen. Albert Sidney Johnston and his army when they marched west from Fort Leavenworth to suppress the "Mormon War" of 1857-58.

For about three hundred miles out of Fort Kearney, the trail followed the prairies; for two thirds of this distance, it clung to the south bank of the Platte, passing through Plum Creek and Midway[3]. At Cottonwood Springs the junction of the North and South branches of the Platte was reached. From here the course moved steadily westward, through Fremont's Springs, O'Fallon's Bluffs, Alkali, Beauvais Ranch, and Diamond Springs to Julesburg, on the South fork of the Platte. Here the stream was forded and the rider then followed the course of Lodge Pole Creek in a northwesterly direction to Thirty Mile Ridge. Thence he journeyed to Mud Springs, Court-House Rock, Chimney Rock, and Scott's Bluffs to Fort Laramie. From this point he passed through the foot-hills to the base of the Rockies, then over the mountains through South Pass and to Fort Bridger. Then to Salt Lake City, Camp Floyd, Ruby Valley, Mountain Wells, across the Humboldt River in Nevada to Bisbys', Carson City, and to Placerville, California; thence to Folsom and Sacramento. Here the mail was taken by a fast steamer down the Sacramento River to San Francisco.

A large part of this route traversed the wildest regions of the Continent. Along the entire course there were but four military posts and they were strung along at intervals of from two hundred and fifty to three hundred and fifty miles from each other. Over most of the journey there were only small way stations to break the awful monotony. Topographically, the trail covered nearly six hundred miles of rolling prairie, intersected here and there by streams fringed with timber. The nature of the mountainous regions, the deserts, and alkali plains as avenues of horseback travel is well understood. Throughout these areas the men and horses had to endure such risks as rocky chasms, snow slides, and treacherous streams, as well as storms of sand and snow. The worst part of the journey lay between Salt Lake City and Sacramento, where for several hundred miles the route ran through a desert, much of it a bed of alkali dust where no living creature could long survive. It was not merely these dangers of dire exposure and privation that threatened, for wherever the country permitted of human life, Indians abounded. From the Platte River valley westward, the old route sped over by the Pony Express is today substantially that of the Union Pacific and Southern Pacific Railroads.

In California, the region most benefited by the express, the opening of the line was likewise awaited with the keenest anticipation. Of course there had been at the outset a few dissenting opinions, the gist of the opposing sentiment being that the Indians would make the operation of the route impossible. One newspaper went so far as to say that it was "Simply inviting slaughter upon all the foolhardy young men who had been engaged as riders". But the California spirit would not down. A vast majority of the people favored the enterprise and clamored for it; and before the express had been long in operation, all classes were united in the conviction that they could not do without it.

At San Francisco and Sacramento, then the two most important towns in the far West, great preparations were made to celebrate the first outgoing and incoming mails. On April 3rd, at the same hour the express started from St. Joseph[4], the eastbound mail was placed on board a steamer at San Francisco and sent up the river, accompanied by an enthusiastic delegation of business men. On the arrival of the pouch and its escort at Sacramento, the capital city, they were greeted with the blare of bands, the firing of guns, and the clanging of gongs. Flags were unfurled and floral decorations lined the streets. That night the first rider for the East, Harry Roff, left the city on a white broncho. He rode the first twenty miles in fifty-nine minutes, changing mounts once. He next took a fresh horse at Folsom and pushed on fifty-five miles farther to Placerville. Here he was relieved by "Boston," who carried the mail to Friday Station, crossing the Sierras en route. Next came Sam Hamilton who rode through Geneva, Carson City, Dayton, and Reed's Station to Fort Churchill, seventy-five miles in all. This point, one hundred and eighty-five miles out of Sacramento had been reached in fifteen hours and twenty minutes, in spite of the Sierra Divide where the snow drifts were thirty feet deep and where the Company had to keep a drove of pack mules moving in order to keep the passageway clear. From Fort Churchill into Ruby Valley went H. J. Faust; from Ruby Valley to Shell Creek the courier was "Josh" Perkins; then came Jim Gentry who carried the mail to Deep Creek, and he was followed by "Let" Huntington who pushed on to Simpson's Springs. From Simpson's to Camp Floyd rode John Fisher, and from the latter place Major Egan carried the mail into Salt Lake City, arriving April 7, at 11:45 P. M.[5] The obstacles to fast travel had been numerous because of snow in the mountains, and stormy spring weather with its attendant discomfort and bad going. Yet the schedule had been maintained, and the last seventy-five miles into Salt Lake City had been ridden in five hours and fifteen minutes.

At that time Placerville and Carson City were the terminals of a local telegraph line. News had been flashed back from Carson on April 4 that the rider had passed that point safely. After that came an anxious wait until April 12 when the arrival of the west-bound express announced that all was well.

The first trip of the Pony Express westbound from St. Joseph to Sacramento was made in nine days and twenty-three hours. East-bound, the run was covered in eleven days and twelve hours. The average time of these two performances was barely half that required by the Butterfield stage over the Southern route. The pony had clipped ten full days from the schedule of its predecessor, and shown that it could keep its schedule - which was as follows:

From St. Joseph to Salt Lake City - 124 hours.

From Salt Lake City to Carson City - 218 hours, from starting point.

From Carson City to Sacramento - 232 hours, from starting point.

From Sacramento to San Francisco - 240 hours, from starting point.

From the very first trip, expressions of genuine appreciation of the new service were shown all along the line. The first express which reached Salt Lake City eastbound on the night of April 7, led the Deseret News, the leading paper of that town to say that: "Although a telegraph is very desirable, we feel well-satisfied with this achievement for, the present." Two days later, the first west-bound express bound from St. Joseph reached the Mormon capital. Oddly enough this rider carried news of an act to amend a bill just proposed in the United States Senate, providing that Utah be organized into Nevada Territory under the name and leadership of the latter[6]. Many of the Mormons, like numerous persons in California, had at first believed the Pony Express an impossibility, but now that it had been demonstrated wholly feasible, they were delighted with its success, whether it brought them good news or bad; for it had brought Utah within six days of the Missouri River and within seven days of Washington City. Prior to this, under the old stage coach régime, the people of that territory had been accustomed to receive their news of the world from six weeks to three months old.

Probably no greater demonstrations were ever held in California cities than when the first incoming express arrived. Its schedule having been announced in the daily papers a week ahead, the people were ready with their welcome. At Sacramento, as when the pony mail had first come up from San Francisco, practically the whole town turned out. Stores were closed and business everywhere suspended. State officials and other citizens of prominence addressed great crowds in commemoration of the wonderful achievement. Patriotic airs were played and sung and no attempt was made to check the merry-making of the populace. After a hurried stop to deliver local mail, the pouch was rushed aboard the fast sailing steamer Antelope, and the trip down the stream begun. Although San Francisco was not reached until the dead of night, the arrival of the express mail was the signal for a hilarious reception. Whistles were blown, bells jangled, and the California Band turned out. The city fire department, suddenly aroused by the uproar, rushed into the street, expecting to find a conflagration, but on recalling the true state of affairs, the firemen joined in with spirit. The express courier was then formally escorted by a huge procession from the steamship dock to the office of the Alta Telegraph, the official Western terminal, and the momentous trip had ended.

The first Pony Express from St. Joseph brought a message of congratulation from President Buchanan to Governor Downey of California, which was first telegraphed to the Missouri River town. It also brought one or two official government communications, some New York, Chicago, and St. Louis newspapers, a few bank drafts, and some business letters addressed to banks and commercial houses in San Francisco - about eighty-five pieces of mail in all[7]. And it had brought news from the East only nine days on the road.

At the outset, the Express reduced the time for letters from New York to the Coast from twenty-three days to about ten days. Before the line had been placed in operation, a telegraph wire, allusion to which has been made, had been strung two hundred and fifty miles Eastward from San Francisco through Sacramento to Carson City, Nevada. Important official business from Washington was therefore wired to St. Joseph, then forwarded by pony rider to Carson City where it was again telegraphed to Sacramento or San Francisco as the case required, thus saving twelve or fifteen hours in transmission on the last lap of the journey. The usual schedule for getting dispatches from the Missouri River to the Coast was eight days, and for letters, ten days.

After the triumphant first trip, when it was fully evident that the Pony Express[8] was a really established enterprise, the St. Joseph Free Democrat broke into the following panegyric:

Take down your map and trace the footprints of our quadrupedantic animal: From St. Joseph on the Missouri to San Francisco, on the Golden Horn - two thousand miles - more than half the distance across our boundless continent; through Kansas, through Nebraska, by Fort Kearney, along the Platte, by Fort Laramie, past the Buttes, over the Rocky Mountains, through the narrow passes and along the steep defiles, Utah, Fort Bridger, Salt Lake City, he witches Brigham with his swift ponyship - through the valleys, along the grassy slopes, into the snow, into sand, faster than Thor's Thialfi, away they go, rider and horse - did you see them? They are in California, leaping over its golden sands, treading its busy streets. The courser has unrolled to us the great American panorama, allowed us to glance at the homes of one million people, and has put a girdle around the earth in forty minutes. Verily the riding is like the riding of Jehu, the son of Nimshi for he rideth furiously. Take out your watch. We are eight days from New York, eighteen from London. The race is to the swift.

The Pony Express had been tried at the tribunal of popular opinion and given a hearty endorsement. It had yet to win the approval of shrewd statesmanship.

Notes:
[2] Root and Connelley's Overland Stage to California.

[3] So called because it was about half way between the Missouri River and Denver.

[4] Reports as to the precise hour of starting do not all agree. It was probably late in the afternoon or early in the evening, no later than 6:30.

[5] Authorities differ somewhat as to the personnel of the first trip; also as to the number of letters carried.

[6] On account of the Mormon outbreak and the troubles of 1857-58, there was at this time much ill-feeling in Congress against Utah. Matters were finally smoothed out and the bill in question was of course dropped. Utah was loyal to the Union throughout the Civil War.

[7] Eastbound the first rider carried about seventy letters.

[8] The idea of a Pony Express was not a new one in 1859. Marco Polo relates that Genghis Khan, ruler of Chinese Tartary had such a courier service about one thousand years ago. This ambitious monarch, it is said, had relay stations twenty-five miles apart, and his riders sometimes covered three hundred miles in twenty-four hours.

About a hundred years back, such a system was in vogue in various countries of Europe.

Early in the nineteenth century before the telegraph was invented, a New York newspaper man named David Hale used a Pony Express system to collect state news. A little later, in 1830, a rival publisher, Richard Haughton, political editor of the

New York Journal of Commerce borrowed the same idea. He afterward founded the Boston Atlas, and by making relays of fast horses and taking advantage of the services offered by a few short lines of railroad then operating in Massachusetts, he was enabled to print election returns by nine o'clock on the morning after election.

This idea was improved by James W. Webb, Editor of the New York Courier and Enquirer, a big daily of that time. In 1832, Webb organized an express rider line between New York and Washington. This undertaking gave his paper much valuable prestige.

In 1833, Hale and Hallock of the Journal of Commerce started a rival line that enabled them to publish Washington news within forty-eight hours, thus giving their paper a big "scoop" over all competitors. Papers in Norfolk, Va., two hundred and twenty-nine miles south-east of Washington actually got the news from the capitol out of the New York Journal of Commerce received by the ocean route, sooner than news printed in Washington could be sent to Norfolk by boat directly down the Potomac River.

The California Pony Express of historic fame was imitated on a small scale in 1861 by the Rocky Mountain News of Denver, then, as now, one of the great newspapers of the West. At that time, this enterprising daily owned and published a paper called the Miner's Record at Tarryall, a mining community some distance out of Denver. The News also had a branch office at Central City, forty-five miles up in the mountains. As soon as information from the War arrived over the California Pony Express and by stage out of old Julesburg from the Missouri River - Denver was not on the Pony Express route - it was hurried to these outlying points by fast horsemen. Thanks to this enterprise, the miners in the heart of the Rockies could get their War news only four days late. - Root and Connelley.

Chapter IV
Operation, Equipment, and Business

On entering the service of the Central Overland California and Pike's Peak Express Company, employees of the Pony Express were compelled to take an oath of fidelity which ran as follows:

"I, - -, do hereby swear, before the Great and Living God, that during my engagement, and while I am an employe of Russell, Majors & Waddell, I will, under no circumstances, use profane language; that I will drink no intoxicating liquors; that I will not quarrel or fight with any other employe of the firm, and that in every respect I will conduct myself honestly, be faithful to my duties, and so direct all my acts as to win the confidence of my employers. So help me God."[9]

It is not to be supposed that all, nor any considerable number of the Pony Express men were saintly, nor that they all took their pledge too seriously. Judged by present-day standards, most of these fellows were rough and unconventional; some of them were bad. Yet one thing is certain: in loyalty and blind devotion to duty, no group of employees will ever surpass the men who conducted the Pony Express. During the sixteen months of its existence, the riders of this wonderful enterprise, nobly assisted by the faithful station-keepers, travelled six hundred and fifty thousand miles, contending against the most desperate odds that a lonely wilderness and savage nature could offer, with the loss of only a single mail. And that mail happened to be of relatively small importance. Only one rider was ever killed outright while on duty. A few were mortally wounded, and occasionally their horses were disabled. Yet with the one exception, they stuck grimly to the saddle or trudged manfully ahead without a horse until the next station was reached. With these men, keeping the schedule came to be a sort of religion, a performance that must be accomplished - even though it forced them to play a desperate game the stakes of which were life and death. Many station men and numbers of riders while off duty were murdered by Indians. They were martyrs to the cause of patriotism and a newer and better civilization. Yet they were hirelings, working for good wages and performing their duties in a simple, matter-of-fact way. Their heroism was never a self-conscious trait.

The riders were young men, seldom exceeding one hundred and twenty-five pounds in weight. Youthfulness, nerve, a wide experience on the frontier and general adaptability were the chief requisites for the Pony Express business. Some of the greatest frontiersmen of the latter 'sixties and the 'seventies were trained in this service, either as pony riders or station men. The latter had even a more dangerous task, since in their isolated shacks they were often completely at the mercy of Indians.

That only one rider was ever taken by the savages was due to the fact that the pony men rode magnificent horses which invariably outclassed the Indian ponies in speed and endurance. The lone man captured while on duty was completely surrounded by a large number of savages on the Platte River in Nebraska. He was shot dead and though his body was not found for several days, his pony, bridled and saddled, escaped safely with the mail which was duly forwarded to its destination. That far more riders were killed or injured while off duty than when in the saddle was due solely to the wise precaution of the Company in selecting such high-grade riding stock. And it took the best of horseflesh to make the schedule.

The riders dressed as they saw fit. The average costume consisted of a buckskin shirt, ordinary trousers tucked into high leather boots, and a slouch hat or cap. They always went armed. At first a Spencer carbine was carried strapped to the rider's back, besides a sheath knife at his side. In the saddle holsters he carried a pair of Colt's revolvers. After a time the carbines were left off and only side arms taken along. The carrying of larger guns meant extra weight, and it was made a rule of the Company that a rider should never fight unless compelled to do so. He was to depend wholly upon speed for safety. The record of the service fully justified this policy.

While the horses were of the highest grade, they were of mixed breed and were purchased over a wide range of territory. Good results were obtained from blooded animals from the Missouri Valley, but considerable preference was shown for the western-bred mustangs. These animals were about fourteen hands high and averaged less than nine hundred pounds in weight. A former blacksmith for the Company who was at one time located at Seneca, Kansas, recalls that one of these native ponies often had to be thrown and staked down with a rope tied to each foot before it could be shod. Then, before the smith could pare the hoofs and nail on the shoes, it was necessary for one man to sit astride the animal's head, and another on its body, while the beast continued to struggle and squeal. To shoe one of these animals often required a half day of strenuous work.

As might be expected, the horse as well as rider traveled very light. The combined weight of the saddle, bridle and saddle bags did not exceed thirteen pounds. The saddle-bag used by the pony rider for carrying mail was called a mochila; it had openings in the center so it would fit snugly over the horn and tree of the saddle and yet be removable without delay. The mochila had four pockets called cantinas in each of its corners one in front and one behind each of the rider's legs. These cantinas held the mail. All were kept carefully locked and three were opened en route only at military posts - Forts Kearney, Laramie, Bridger, Churchill and at Salt Lake City. The fourth pocket was for the local or way mail-stations. Each local station-keeper had a key and could open it when necessary. It held a time-card on which a record of the arrival and departure at the various stations where it was opened, was kept. Only one mochila was used on a trip; it was transferred by the rider from one horse to another until the destination was reached.

Letters were wrapped in oil silk to protect them from moisture, either from stormy weather, fording streams, or perspiring animals. While a mail of twenty pounds might be carried, the average weight did not exceed fifteen pounds. The postal charges were at first, five dollars for each half-ounce letter, but this rate was afterward reduced by the Post Office Department to one dollar for each half ounce. At this figure it remained as long as the line was in business. In addition to this rate, a regulation government envelope costing ten cents, had to be purchased. Patrons generally made use of a specially light tissue paper for their correspondence. The large newspapers of New York, Boston, Chicago, St. Louis, and San Francisco were among the best customers of the service. Some of the Eastern dailies even kept special correspondents at St. Joseph to receive and telegraph to the home office news from the West as soon as it arrived. On account of the enormous postage rates these newspapers would print special editions of Civil War news on the thinnest of paper to avoid all possible mailing bulk.

Mr. Frank A. Root of Topeka, Kansas, who was Assistant Postmaster and Chief Clerk in the post office at Atchison during the last two months of the line's existence, in 1861, says that during that period the Express, which was running semi-weekly, brought about three hundred and fifty letters each trip from California[10]. Many of these communications were from government and state officials in California and Oregon, and addressed to the Federal authorities at Washington, particularly to Senators and Representatives from these states and to authorities of the War Department. A few were addressed to Abraham Lincoln, President of the United States. A large number of these letters were from business and professional men in Portland, San Francisco, Oakland, and Sacramento, and mailed to firms in the large cities of the East and Middle West. Not to mention the rendering of invaluable help to the Government in retaining California at the beginning of the War, the Pony Express was of the greatest importance to the commercial interests of the West.

The line was frequently used by the British Government in forwarding its Asiatic correspondence to London. In 1860, a report of the activities of the English fleet off the coast of China was sent through from San Francisco eastward over this route. For the transmission of these dispatches that Government paid one hundred and thirty-five dollars Pony Express charges.

Nor did the commercial houses of the Pacific Coast cities appear to mind a little expense in forwarding their business letters. Mr. Root says there would often be twenty-five one dollar "Pony" stamps and the same number of Government stamps - a total in postage of twenty-seven dollars and fifty cents - on a single envelope. Not much frivolity passed through these mails.

Pony Express riders received an average salary of from one hundred dollars to one hundred and twenty-five dollars a month. A few whose rides were particularly dangerous or who had braved unusual dangers received one hundred and fifty dollars. Station men and their assistants were paid from fifty to one hundred dollars monthly.

Of the eighty riders usually in the service, half were always riding in either direction, East and West. The average "run" was seventy-five miles, the men going and coming over their respective divisions on each succeeding day. Yet there were many exceptions to this rule, as will be shown later. At the outset, although facilities for shorter relays had been provided, it was planned to run each horse twenty-five miles with an average of three horses to the rider; but it was soon found that a horse could rarely continue at a maximum speed for so great a distance. Consequently, it soon became the practice to change mounts every ten or twelve miles or as nearly that as possible. The exact distance was governed largely by the nature of the country. While this shortening of the relay necessitated transferring the mochila many more times on each trip, it greatly facilitated the schedule; for it was at once seen that the average horse or pony in the Express service could be crowded to the limit of its speed over the reduced distance.

One of the station-keeper's most important duties was to have a fresh horse saddled and bridled a half hour before the Express was due. Only two minutes time was allowed for changing mounts. The rider's approach was watched for with keen anxiety. By daylight he could generally be seen in a cloud of dust, if in the desert or prairie regions. If in the mountains, the clear air made it possible for the station men to detect his approach a long way off, provided there were no obstructions to hide the view. At night the rider would make his presence known by a few lusty whoops. Dashing up to the station, no time was wasted. The courier would already have loosed his mochila, which he tossed ahead for the keeper to adjust on the fresh horse, before dismounting. A sudden reining up of his foam-covered steed, and "All's well along the road, Hank!" to the station boss, and he was again mounted and gone, usually fifteen seconds after his arrival. Nor was there any longer delay when a fresh rider took up the "run."

Situated at intervals of about two hundred miles were division points[11] in charge of locally important agents or superintendents. Here were kept extra men, animals, and supplies as a precaution against the raids of Indians, desperadoes, or any emergency likely to arise. Division agents had considerable authority; their pay was as good as that received by the best riders. They were men of a heroic and even in some instances, desperate character, in spite of their oath of service. In certain localities much infested with horse thievery and violence it was necessary to have in charge men of the fight-the-devil-with-fire type in order to keep the business in operation. Noted among this class of Division agents, with headquarters at the Platte Crossing near Fort Kearney, was Jack Slade[12], who, though a good servant of the Company, turned out to be one of the worst "bad" men in the history of the West. He had a record of twenty-six "killings" to his credit, but he kept his Division thoroughly purged of horse thieves and savage marauders, for he knew how to "get" his man whenever there was trouble.

The schedule was at first fixed at ten days for eight months of the year and twelve days during the winter season, but this was soon lowered to eight and ten days respectively. An average speed of ten miles an hour including stops had to be maintained on the summer schedule. In the winter the run was sustained at eight miles an hour; deep snows made the latter performance the more difficult of the two.

The best record made by the Pony Express was in getting President Lincoln's inaugural speech across the continent in March, 1861. This address, outlining as it did the attitude of the new Chief Executive toward the pending conflict, was anticipated with the deepest anxiety by the people on the Pacific Coast. Evidently inspired by the urgency of the situation, the Company determined to surpass all performances. Horses were led out, in many cases, two or three miles from the stations, in order to meet the incoming riders and to secure the supreme limit of speed and endurance on this momentous trip. The document was carried through from St. Joseph to Sacramento - 1966 miles - in just seven days and seventeen hours, an average speed of ten and six-tenths miles an hour. And this by flesh and blood, pounding the dirt over the plains, mountains, and deserts! The best individual performance on this great run was by "Pony Bob" Haslam who galloped the one hundred and twenty miles from Smith's Creek to Fort Churchill in eight hours and ten minutes, an average of fourteen and seven-tenths miles per hour. On this record-breaking trip the message was carried the six hundred and seventy-five miles between St. Joseph and Denver[13] in sixty-nine hours; the last ten miles of this leg of the journey being ridden in thirty-one minutes. Today, but few overland express trains, hauled by giant locomotives over heavy steel rails on a rock-ballasted roadbed average more than thirty miles per hour between the Missouri and the Pacific Coast.

The news of the election of Lincoln in November 1860, and President Buchanan's last message a month later were carried through in eight days.

Late in the winter and early in the spring of 1861, just prior to the beginning of the war, many good records were made with urgent Government dispatches.

News of the firing upon Fort Sumter was taken through in eight days and fourteen hours. From then on, while the Pony Express service continued, the business men and public officials of California began giving prize money to the Company, to be awarded those riders who made the best time carrying war news. On one occasion they raised a purse of three hundred dollars for the star rider when a pouch containing a number of Chicago papers full of information from the South arrived at Sacramento a day ahead of schedule.

That these splendid achievements could never have been attained without a wonderful degree of enthusiasm and loyalty on the part of the men, scarcely needs asserting. The pony riders were highly respected by the stage and freight employees - in fact by all respectable men throughout the West. Nor were they honored merely for what they did; they were the sort of men who command respect. To assist a rider in any way was deemed a high honor; to do aught to retard him was the limit of wrong-doing, a woeful offense. On the first trip west-bound, the rider between Folsom and Sacramento was thrown, receiving a broken leg. Shortly after the accident, a Wells Fargo stage happened along, and a special agent of that Company, who chanced to be a passenger, seeing the predicament, volunteered to finish the run. This he did successfully, reaching Sacramento only ninety minutes late. Such instances are typical of the manly cooperation that made the Pony Express the true success that it was.

Mark Twain, who made a trip across the continent in 1860 has left this glowing account[14] of a pony and rider that he saw while traveling overland in a stage coach:

We had a consuming desire from the beginning, to see a pony rider; but somehow or other all that passed us, and all that met us managed to streak by in the night and so we heard only a whiz and a hail, and the swift phantom of the desert was gone before we could get our heads out of the windows. But now we were expecting one along every moment, and would see him in broad daylight. Presently the driver exclaims:

"Here he comes!"

Every neck is stretched further and every eye strained wider away across the endless dead level of the prairie, a black speck appears against the sky, and it is plain that it moves. Well I should think so! In a second it becomes a horse and rider, rising and falling, rising and falling - sweeping toward us nearer and nearer growing more and more distinct, more and more sharply defined - nearer and still nearer, and the flutter of hoofs comes faintly to the ear - another instant a whoop and a hurrah from our upper deck, a wave of the rider's hands but no reply and man and horse burst past our excited faces and go winging away like the belated fragment of a storm!

So sudden is it all, and so like a flash of unreal fancy, that but for a flake of white foam left quivering and perishing on a mail sack after the vision had flashed by and disappeared, we might have doubted whether we had seen any actual horse and man at all, maybe.

Notes:

[9] This was the same pledge which the original firm had required of its men. Both Russell, Majors, and Waddell, and the C. O. C. and P. P. Exp. Co., which they incorporated, adhered to a rigid observance of the Sabbath. They insisted on their men doing as little work as possible on that day, and had them desist from work whenever possible. And they stuck faithfully to these policies. Probably no concern ever won a higher and more deserved reputation for integrity in the fulfillment of its contracts and for business reliability than Russell, Majors, and Waddell.

[10] Exact figures are not obtainable for the west bound mail but it was probably not so heavy.

At this time - Sept., 1861 - the telegraph had been extended from the Missouri to Fort Kearney, Nebraska, and letter pouches from the Pony Express were sent by overland stage from Kearney to Atchison. Messages of grave concern were wired as soon as this station was reached.

[11] These were executive divisions and not to be confused with the riders' divisions. The latter were merely the stations separating each man's "run."

[12] Slade was afterward hanged by vigilantes in Virginia City, Montana. The authentic story of his life surpasses in romance and tragedy most of the pirate tales of fiction.

[13] The dispatch was taken from the main line to the Colorado capital by special service. Denver, it will be remembered, was not on the regular "Pony route," which ran north of that city. There was then no telegraph in operation west of the

Missouri River in Kansas or Nebraska.

[14] Roughing It.

Chapter V
California and the Secession Menace

When the Southern states withdrew, a conspiracy was on foot to force California out of the Union, and organize a new Republic of the Pacific with the Sierra Madre and the Rocky Mountains for its Eastern boundary. This proposed commonwealth, when once erected, and when it had subjugated all Union men in the West who dared oppose it, would eventually unite with the Confederacy; and in event of the latter's success - which at the opening of the war to many seemed certain - the territory of the Confederate States of America would embrace the entire Southwest, and stretch from the Atlantic to the Pacific. Aside from its general plans, the exact details of this plot are of course impossible to secure. But that the conspiracy existed has never been disproved.

That the rebel sympathizers in California were plotting, as soon as the War began, to take the Presidio at the entrance to the Golden Gate, together with the forts on Alcatraz Island, the Custom House, the Mint, the Post Office, and all United States property, and then having made the formation of their Republic certain, invade the Mexican State of Sonora and annex it to the new commonwealth, has never been gainsaid. That these conspiracies existed and were held in grave seriousness is revealed by the official correspondence of that time. That they had been fomenting for many months is apparently revealed by this additional fact: during Buchanan's administration, John B. Floyd, a southern man who gave up his position to fight for the Confederacy, was Secretary of War. When the Rebellion started, it was found[15] that Floyd, while in office, had removed 135,430 firearms, together with much ammunition and heavy ordnance, from the big Government arsenal at Springfield, Massachusetts, and distributed them at various points in the South and Southwest. Of this number, fifty thousand[16] were sent to California where twenty-five thousand muskets had already been stored. And all this was done underhandedly, without the knowledge of Congress.

California was unfortunate in having as a representative in the United States Senate at this time, William Gwin, also a man of southern birth who had cast his fortunes in the Golden State at the outset, when the gold boom was on. Until secession was imminent, Gwin served his adopted state well enough. His encouragement of the Pony Express enterprise has already been pointed out. It is doubtful if he were statesman enough to have foreseen the significant part this organization was to play in the early stages of the War. Otherwise his efforts in its behalf must have been lacking - though the careers of political adventurers like Gwin are full of strange inconsistencies[17].

Speaking in the Senate, on December 12, 1859, Gwin declared, that he believed that "all slave holding states of this confederacy can establish a separate and independent government that will be impregnable to the assaults of all foreign enemies." He further went on to show that they had the power to do it, and asserted that if the southern states went out of the Union, "California would be with the South." Then, as a convincing proof of his duplicity, he had these pro-rebel statements stricken from the official report of his speech, that his constituents might not take fright, and perhaps spoil some of the designs which he and his scheming colleagues had upon California. Of course these remarks reached the ears of his constituents anyhow, and though prefaced by a studied evasiveness on his part, they contributed much to the feeling of unrest and insecurity that then prevailed along the Coast.

It is of course a well-known fact that California never did secede, and that soon after the war began, she swung definitely and conclusively into the Union column. The danger of secession was wholly potential. Yet potential dangers are none the less real. Had it not been for the determined energies of a few loyalists in California, led by General E. A. Sumner and cooperating with the Federal Government by means of the swiftest communication then possible - the Pony Express - history today, might read differently.

Now to turn once more to the potential dangers[18] that made the California crisis a reality. About three-eighths of the population were of southern descent and solidly united in sympathy for the Confederate states. This vigorous minority included upwards of sixteen thousand Knights of the Golden Circle, a pro-Confederate secret organization that was active and dangerous in all the doubtful states in winning over to the southern cause those who feebly protested loyalty to the Union but who opposed war. Many of these "knights" were prosperous and substantial citizens who, working under the guise of their local respectability, exerted a profound influence. Here then, at the outset, was a vigorous and not a small minority, whose influence was greatly out of proportion to their numbers because of their zeal; and who would have seized the balance of power unless held in check by an aroused Union sentiment and military intimidation.

Another class of men to be feared was a small but powerful group representing much wealth, a financial class which proverbially shuns war because of the expense which war involves; a class that always insists upon peace, even at the cost of compromised honor. These men, with the influence which their money commanded, would inevitably espouse the side that seemed the most likely of speedy success; and in view of the early successes of the Confederate armies and the zealous proselytizing of rebel sympathizers in their midst they were a potential risk to loyal California.

The native Spanish or Mexican classes then numerically strong in that state, were appealed to by the anti-Unionists from various cunning approaches, chief of which was the theory that the many real estate troubles and complicated land titles by which they had been annoyed since the separation from Old Mexico in 1847, would be promptly adjusted under Confederate authority. While nearly all these natives were ignorant, many held considerable property and they in turn influenced their poorer brethren. Chimerical as this argument may sound, it had much weight.

Another group of persons also large potentially and a serious menace when proselyted by the apostles of rebellion, were the squatters and trespassers who were occupying land to which they had no lawful right. Many of these men were reckless; some had already been entangled in the courts because of their false land claims. Hence their attitude toward the existing Government was ugly and defiant. Yet they were now assured that they might remain on their lands forever undisturbed, under a rebel régime.

Added to all these sources of danger was the attitude of the thousands of well-meaning people - who, regardless of rebel solicitation, were at first indifferent. They thought that the great distance which separated them from the seat of war made it a matter of but little importance whether California aroused herself or not. They were of course counseling neutrality as the easiest way of avoiding trouble.

Turning now to the forces, moral, military, and political, that were working to save California - first there was a loyal newspaper press, which saw and followed its duty with unflinching devotion. It firmly held before the people the loyal responsibility of the state and declared that the ties of union were too sacred to be broken. It was the moral duty of the people to remain loyal. It truthfully asserted that California's influence in the Federal Union should be an example for other states to follow. If the idea of a Pacific Republic were repudiated by their own citizens, such action would discourage secession elsewhere and be a great moral handicap to that movement. And the press further pointed out with convincing clearness, that should the Union be dissolved, the project for a Pacific Railroad[19] with which the future of the Commonwealth was inevitably committed, would likely fail.

Aroused by the moral importance of its position, the state legislature, early in the winter of 1860-1861, had passed a resolution of fidelity to the Union, in which it declared "That California is ready to maintain the rights and honor of the National Government at home and abroad, and at all times to respond to any requisitions that may be made upon her to defend the Republic against foreign or domestic foes." Succeeding events proved the genuineness of this resolve.

In the early spring of 1861, the War Department sent General Edwin A. Sumner to take command of the Military Department of the Pacific with headquarters at San Francisco, supplanting General Albert Sidney Johnston who resigned to fight for the South. This was a most fortunate appointment, as Sumner proved a resourceful and capable official, ideally suited to meet the crisis before him. Nor does this reflect in any way upon the superb soldierly qualities of his predecessor. Johnston was no doubt too manly an officer to take part in the romantic conspiracies about him. He was every inch a brave soldier who did his fighting in the open. Like Robert E. Lee, he joined the Confederacy in conscientious good faith, and he met death bravely at Shiloh in April, 1862.

Sumner was a man of action and he faced the situation squarely. To him, California and the nation will always be indebted. One of his first decisive acts was to check the secession movement in Southern California by placing a strong detachment of soldiers at Los Angeles. This force proved enough to stop any incipient uprisings in that part of the state. Some of the disturbing element in this district then moved over into Nevada where cooperation was made with the pro-Confederate men there. The Nevada rebel faction had made considerable headway by assuring unsuspecting persons that it was acting on the authority of the Confederate Government. On June 5, 1861, the rebel flag was unfurled at Virginia City. Again Sumner acted. He immediately sent a Federal force to garrison Fort Churchill, and a body of men under Major Blake and Captain Moore seized all arms found in the possession of suspected persons. A rebel militia company with four hundred men enrolled and one hundred under arms was found and dispersed by the Federals. This decisive action completely stopped any uprisings across the state line, uprisings which might easily have spread into California.

In the meantime, under General Sumner's direction, soldiers had been enlisted and were being rapidly drilled for any emergency. The War Department, on being advised of this available force, at once sent the following dispatch, which, with those that follow are typical of the correspondence which the Pony Express couriers were now rushing across the Continent toward and from Washington.

Telegraph and Pony Express. Adjutant-General's Office.

Washington, July 24, 1861. Brigadier General Sumner, Commanding Department of the Pacific.

One regiment of infantry and five companies of cavalry have been accepted from California to aid in protecting the overland mail route via Salt Lake.

Please detail officers to muster these troops into service. Blanks will be sent by steamer.

By order: George D. Ruggles. Assistant Adjutant General.

While recognizing the great need of extending proper military protection to the mail route, it must have been disheartening to Sumner and the loyalists to see this force ordered into service outside the state. For now, late in the summer of 1861, the time of national crisis - the Californian trouble was approaching its climax. On July 20, the Union army had been beaten at Bull Run and driven back, a rabble of fugitives, into the panic stricken capital. Then came weeks and months of delay and uncertainty while the overcautious McClellan sought to build up a new military machine. The entire North was overspread with gloom; the Confederates were jubilant and full of self-confidence. In California the psychological situation was similar but even more acute, for encouraged by Confederate success, the rebel faction became bolder than ever, and openly planned to win the state election to be held on September 4. If successful at the polls, the reins of organized political power would pass into its hands and a secession convention would be a direct possibility. And to intensify the danger was the confirmed indifference or stubbornness of many citizens who seemed to place petty personal differences before the interests of the state and nation at large.

As is well known, Lincoln and the Federal Government accepted the defeat at Bull Run calmly, and set about with grim determination to whip the South at any cost. The President asked Congress for four hundred thousand men and was voted five hundred thousand. In pursuance of such policies, these urgent dispatches were hurried across the country:

War Department. Washington, August 14, 1861. Hon. John G. Downey,

Governor of California, Sacramento City, Cal.

Please organize, equip, and have mustered into service, at the earliest date possible, four regiments of infantry and one regiment of cavalry, to be placed at the disposal of General Sumner.

Simon Cameron, Secretary of War.

By telegraph to Fort Kearney and thence by Pony Express and telegraph.

War Department, August 15, 1861. Hon. John G. Downey,

Governor of California, Sacramento City, Cal.

In filling the requisition given you August 14th, for five regiments, please make General J. H. Carleton of San Francisco, colonel of a cavalry regiment, and give him proper authority to organize as promptly as possible.

Simon Cameron, Secretary of War.

Telegraph and Pony Express and telegraph.

The work of enlisting the five thousand men thus requisitioned was carried forward with great rapidity. Within two weeks, on the 28th, the Pony Express brought word that the War Department was about to order this force overland into Texas, to act, no doubt, as a barrier to the advancing Confederate armies who were then planning an invasion of New Mexico as the first decisive step in carrying the conflict into the heart of the Southwest. It was understood, further, that General Sumner would be ordered to vacate his position as Commander of the Department of the Pacific and lead his recruits into the service.

To the authorities at Washington, a campaign of aggression with western troops had no doubt seemed the best means of defending California and adjacent territory from Confederate attack. To the Unionists of California, the report that their troops and Sumner were to leave the state spelt extreme discouragement. They had felt some degree of hope and security so long as organized forces were in their midst, and the presence of Sumner everywhere inspired confidence among discouraged patriots. To be deprived of their soldiers was bad enough; to lose Sumner was intolerable. Accordingly, a formal petition protesting against this action, was drawn up, addressed to the War Department, and signed by important firms and prominent business men of San Francisco[20].

In this petition they said among other things, that the War Department probably was not aware of the real state of affairs in California, and they openly requested that the order, be rescinded. They declared that a majority of the California State officers were out-and-out secessionists and that the others were at least hostile to the administration and would accept a peace policy at any sacrifice. They were suspicious of the Governor's loyalty and declared that, "Every appointment made by our Governor within the last three months, unmistakably indicates his entire sympathy and cooperation with those plotting to sever California from her allegiance to the Union, and that, too, at the hazard of Civil War."[21]

Continuing at detailed length, the petitioners spoke of the great effort being put forth by the secession element to win the forthcoming election. Whereas their opponents were united, the Union party was divided into a Douglas and a Republican faction. Should the anti-Unionists triumph, they declared there were reasons to expect not merely the loss of California to the Union ranks but internecine strife and fratricidal murders such as were then ravaging the Missouri and Kansas border.

The petition then pointed out the truly great importance of California to the Union, and asserted that no precaution leading to the preservation of her loyalty should be overlooked. It was a thousand times easier to retain a state in allegiance than to overcome disloyalty disguised as state authority. The best way to check treasonable activities was to convince traitors of their helplessness. The petitioners further declared that to deprive California of needed United States military support just then, would be a direct encouragement to traitors. An ounce of precaution was worth a pound of cure.

The loyalists triumphed in the state election on September 4, 1861, and on that date the California crisis was safely passed. The contest, to be sure, had revealed about twenty thousand anti-Union voters in the state, but the success of the Union faction restored their feeling of self-confidence. The pendulum had at last swung safely in the right direction, and henceforth California could be and was reckoned as a loyal asset to the Union. Such expressions of disloyalty as her secessionists continued to disclose, were of a sporadic and flimsy nature, never materializing into a formidable sentiment; and, adding to their discouragement, the failure of the Confederate invasion of New Mexico in 1862, was no doubt an important factor in suppressing any further open desires for secession.

Sumner was not called East until the October following the election. His removal of course caused keen regret along the coast; but Colonel George Wright, his successor in charge of the Department of the Pacific, proved a masterful man and in every way equal to the situation. In the long run, Colonel Wright probably was as satisfactory to the loyal people of California as General Sumner had been. The five thousand troops were not detailed for duty in the South. Like the first detachment of fifteen hundred, their efforts were directed mainly to protecting the overland mails and guarding the frontier[22].

Throughout this crisis, news was received twice a week by the Pony Express, and, be it remembered, in less than half the time required by the old stage coach. Of its services then, no better words can be used than those of Hubert Howe Bancroft.

It was the pony to which every one looked for deliverance; men prayed for the safety of the little beast, and trembled lest the service should be discontinued. Telegraphic dispatches from Washington and New York were sent to St. Louis and thence to Fort Kearney, whence the pony brought them to Sacramento where they were telegraphed to San Francisco.

Great was the relief of the people when Hole's bill for a daily mail service was passed and the service changed from the Southern to the Central route, as it was early in the summer. * * * Yet after all, it was to the flying pony that all eyes and hearts were turned.

The Pony Express was a real factor in the preservation of California to the Union.

Notes:

[15] Bancroft.

[16] lbid.

[17] After the War had started, Gwin deserted California and the Union and joined the Confederacy. When this power was broken up, he fled to Mexico and entered the service of Maximilian, then puppet emperor of that unfortunate country. Maximilian bestowed an abundance of hollow honors upon the renegade senator, and made him Duke of the Province of Sonora, which region Gwin and his clique had doubtless coveted as an integral part of their projected "Republic of the Pacific." Because of this empty title, the nickname, "Duke," was ever afterward given him. When Maximilian's soap bubble monarchy had disappeared, Gwin finally returned to California where he passed his old age in retirement.

[18] Senate documents.

[19] All parties in California were unanimous in their desire for a transcontinental railroad. No political faction there could receive any support unless it strongly endorsed this project.

[20] The signers of this petition were: Robert C. Rogers, Macondray & Co., Jno. Sime & Co., J. B. Thomas, W. W. Stow, Horace P. James, Geo. F. Bragg & Co., Flint, Peabody & Co., Wm. B. Johnston, D. O. Mills, H. M. Newhall & Co., Henry Schmildell, Murphy Grant & Co., Wm. T. Coleman & Co., DeWitt Kittle & Co., Richard M. Jessup, Graves Williams & Buckley, Donohoe, Ralston & Co., H. M. Nuzlee, Geo. C. Shreve & Co., Peter Danahue, Kellogg, Hewston & Co., Moses Ellis & Co., R. D. W. Davis & Co., L. B. Beuchley & Co., Wm. A. Dana, Jones, Dixon & Co., J. Y. Halleck & Co., Forbes & Babcock, A. T. Lawton, Geo. J. Brooks & Co., Jno. B. Newton & Co., Chas. W. Brooks & Co., James Patrick & Co., Locke & Montague, Janson, Bond & Co., Jennings & Brewster, Treadwell & Co., William Alvord & Co., Shattuck & Hendley, Randall & Jones, J. B. Weir & Co., B. C. Hand & Co., O. H. Giffin & Bro., Dodge & Shaw, Tubbs & Co., J. Whitney, Jr., C. Adolph Low & Co.,

Haynes & Lawton, J. D. Farnell, C. E. Hitchcock, Geo. Howes & Co., Sam Merritt, Jacob Underhill & Co., Morgan Stone & Co., J. W. Brittan, T. H. & J. S. Bacon, R. B. Swain & Co., Fargo & Co., Nathaniel Page, Stevens Baker & Co., A. E. Brewster & Co., Fay, Brooks & Backus, Wm. Norris, and E. H. Parker.

(Above data taken from Government Secret Correspondence. Ordered printed by the second session of the 50th Congress in 1889, Senate Document No. 70.)

[21] In the writer's judgment, these charges against Governor Downey were prejudicial and unjust.

[22] During the War of the Rebellion, California raised 16,231 troops, more than the whole United States army had been at the commencement of hostilities. Practically all these soldiers were assigned to routine and patrol duty in the far West, such as keeping down Indian revolts, and garrisoning forts, as a defense against any uprising of Indians, or protection against Confederate invasion. The exceptions were the California Hundred, and the California Four Hundred, volunteer detachments who went East of their own accord and won undying honors in the thick of the struggle.

Chapter VI
Riders and Famous Rides

Bart Riles, the pony rider, died this morning from wounds received at Cold Springs, May 16.

The men at Dry Creek Station have all been killed and it is thought those at Robert's Creek have met with the same fate.

Six Pike's Peakers found the body of the station keeper horribly mutilated, the station burned, and all the stock missing from Simpson's.

Eight horses were stolen from Smith's Creek on last Monday, supposedly by road agents.

The above are random extracts from frontier newspapers, printed while the Pony Express was running. The Express could never have existed on its high plane of efficiency, without an abundance of coolheaded, hardened men; men who knew not fear and who were expert - though sometimes in vain - in all the wonderful arts of self-preservation practiced on the old frontier. That these employees could have performed even the simplest of their duties, without stirring and almost incredible adventures, it is needless to assert.

The faithful relation of even a considerable number of the thrilling experiences to which the "Pony" men were subjected would discount fiction. Yet few of these adventures have been recorded. Today, after a lapse of over fifty years, nearly all of the heroes who achieved them have gone out on that last long journey from which no man returns. While history can pay the tribute of preserving some anecdotes of them and their collective achievements, it must be forever silent as to many of their personal acts of heroism.

While lasting praise is due the faithful station men who, in their isolation, so often bore the murderous attacks of Indians and bandits, it is, perhaps, to the riders

that the seeker of romance is most likely to turn. It was the riders' skill and forti-
tude that made the operation of the line possible. Both riders and hostlers shared
the same privations, often being reduced to the necessity of eating wolf meat and
drinking foul or brackish water.

While each rider was supposed to average seventy-five miles a trip, riding from
three to seven horses, accidents were likely to occur, and it was not uncommon for
a man to lose his way. Such delays meant serious trouble in keeping the schedule,
keyed up, as it was, to the highest possible speed. It was confronting such emer-
gencies, and in performing the duties of comrades who had been killed or disabled
while awaiting their turns to ride, that the most exciting episodes took place.

Among the more famous riders[23] was Jim Moore who later became a ranch-
man in the South Platte Valley, Nebraska. Moore made his greatest ride on June 8,
1860. He happened to be at Midway Station, half way between the Missouri River
and Denver, when the west-bound messenger arrived with important Government
dispatches to California. Moore "took up the run," riding continuously one hundred
and forty miles to old Julesburg, the end of his division. Here he met the eastbound
messenger, also with important missives, from the Coast to Washington. By all the
rules of the game Moore should have rested a few hours at this point, but his successor, who would have picked up the pouch and started eastward, had been killed
the day before. The mail must go, and the schedule must be sustained. Without
asking any favors of the man who had just arrived from the West, Moore resumed
the saddle, after a delay of only ten minutes, without even stopping to eat, and was
soon pounding eastward on his return trip. He made it, too, in spite of lurking Indians, hunger and fatigue, covering the round trip of two hundred and eighty miles
in fourteen hours and forty-six minutes an average speed of over eighteen miles an
hour. Furthermore, his west-bound mail had gone through from St. Joseph to Sacramento on a record-making run of eight days and nine hours.

William James, always called "Bill" James, was a native of Virginia. He had
crossed the plains with his parents in a wagon train when only five years old. At
eighteen, he was one of the best Pony Express riders in the service. James's route
lay between Simpson's Park and Cole Springs, Nevada, in the Smoky Valley range
of mountains. He rode only sixty miles each way but covered his round trip of one
hundred and twenty miles in twelve hours, including all stops. He always rode

California mustangs, using five of these animals each way. His route crossed the summits of two mountain ridges, lay through the Shoshone Indian country, and was one of the loneliest and most dangerous divisions on the line. Yet "Bill" never took time to think about danger, nor did he ever have any serious trouble.

Theodore Rand rode the Pony Express during the entire period of its organization. His run was from Box Elder to Julesburg, one hundred and ten miles and he made the entire distance both ways by night. His schedule, night run though it was, required a gait of ten miles an hour, but Rand often made it at an average of twelve, thus saving time on the through schedule for some unfortunate rider who might have trouble and delay. Originally, Rand used only four or five horses each way, but this number, in keeping with the revised policy of the Company, was afterward doubled, an extra mount being furnished him every twelve or fifteen miles.

Johnnie Frey who has already been mentioned as the first rider out of St. Joseph, was little more than a boy when he entered the pony service. He was a native Missourian, weighing less than one hundred and twenty-five pounds. Though small in stature, he was every inch a man. Frey's division ran from St. Joseph to Seneca, Kansas, eighty miles, which he covered at an average of twelve and one half miles an hour, including all stops. When the war started, Frey enlisted in the Union army under General Blunt. His short but worthy career was cut short in 1863 when he fell in a hand-to-hand fight with rebel bushwhackers in Arkansas. In this, his last fight, Frey is said to have killed five of his assailants before being struck down.

Jim Beatley, whose real name was Foote, was another Virginian, about twenty-five years of age. He rode on an eastern division, usually west out of Seneca. On one occasion, he traveled from Seneca to Big Sandy, fifty miles and back, doubling his route twice in one week. Beatley was killed by a stage hand in a personal quarrel, the affair taking place on a ranch in Southern Nebraska in 1862.

William Boulton was one of the older riders in the service; his age at that time is given at about thirty-five. Boulton rode for about three months with Beatley[24]. On one occasion, while running between Seneca and Guittards', Boulton's horse gave out when five miles from the latter station. Without a moment's delay, he removed his letter pouch and hurried the mail in on foot, where a fresh horse was at once provided and the schedule resumed.

Melville Baughn, usually known as "Mel," had a pony run between Fort Kearney and Thirty-two-mile Creek. Once while "laying off" between trips, a thief made off with his favorite horse. Scarcely had the miscreant gotten away when Baughn discovered the loss. Hastily saddling another steed, "Mel" gave pursuit, and though handicapped, because the outlaw had the pick of the stable, Baughn's superior horsemanship, even on an inferior mount, soon told. After a chase of several miles, he forced the fellow so hard that he abandoned the stolen animal at a place called Loup Fork, and sneaked away. Recovering the horse, Baughn then returned to his station, found a mail awaiting him, and was off on his run without further delay. With him and his fellow employes, running down a horse thief was but a trifling incident and an annoyance merely because of the bother and delay which it necessitated. Baughn was afterward hanged for murder at Seneca, but his services to the Pony Express were above reproach.

Another Eastern Division man was Jack Keetly, who also rode from St. Joseph to Seneca, alternating at times with Frey and Baughn. Keetley's greatest performance, and one of the most remarkable ever achieved in the service, was riding from Rock Creek to St. Joseph; then back to his starting point and on to Seneca, and from Seneca once more to Rock Creek - three hundred and forty miles without rest. He traveled continuously for thirty-one hours, his entire run being at the rate of eleven miles an hour. During the last five miles of his journey, he fell asleep in the saddle and in this manner concluded his long trip.

Don C. Rising, who afterwards settled in Northern Kansas, was born in Painted Post, Steuben County, New York, in 1844, and came West when thirteen years of age. He rode in the pony service nearly a year, from November, 1860, until the line was abandoned the following October, most of his service being rendered before he was seventeen. Much of his time was spent running eastward out of Fort Kearney until the telegraph had reached that point and made the operation of the Express between the fort and St. Joseph no longer necessary. On two occasions, Rising is said to have maintained a continuous speed of twenty miles an hour while carrying important dispatches between Big Sandy and Rock Creek.

One rider who was well known as "Little Yank" was a boy scarcely out of his teens and weighing barely one hundred pounds. He rode along the Platte River between Cottonwood Springs and old Julesburg and frequently made one hundred miles on a single trip.

Another man named Hogan, of whom little is known, rode northwesterly out of Julesburg across the Platte and to Mud Springs, eighty miles.

Jimmy Clark rode between various stations east of Fort Kearney, usually between Big Sandy and Hollenburg. Sometimes his run took him as far West as Liberty Farm on the Little Blue River.

James W. Brink, or "Dock" Brink as he was known to his associates, was one of the early riders, entering the employ of the Pony Express Company in April, 1860. While "Dock" made a good record as a courier, his chief fame was gained in a fight at Rock Creek station, in which Brink and Wild Bill[25] "cleaned out" the McCandless gang of outlaws, killing five of their number.

Charles Cliff had an eighty-mile pony run when only seventeen years of age, but, like Brink, young Cliff gained his greatest reputation as a fighter, - in his case fighting Indians. It seems that while Cliff was once freighting with a small train of nine wagons, it was attacked by a party of one hundred Sioux Indians and besieged for three days until a larger train approached and drove the redskins away. During the conflict, Cliff received three bullets in his body and twenty-seven in his clothing, but he soon recovered from his injuries, and was afterward none the less valuable to the Pony Express service.

J. G. Kelley, later a citizen of Denver, was a veteran pony man. He entered the employ of the company at the outset, and helped Superintendent Roberts to lay out the route across Nevada. Along the Carson River, tiresome stretches of corduroy road had to be built. Kelley relates that in constructing this highway willow trees were cut near the stream and the trunks cut into the desired lengths before being laid in place. The men often had to carry these timbers in their arms for three hundred yards, while the mosquitoes swarmed so thickly upon their faces and hands as to make their real color and identity hard to determine.

At the Sink of the Carson[26], a great depression of the river on its course through the desert, Kelley assisted in building a fort for protecting the line against Indians. Here there were no rocks nor timber, and so the structure had to be built of adobe mud. To get this mud to a proper consistency, the men tramped it all day with their bare feet. The soil was soaked with alkali, and as a result, according to Kelley's story, their feet were swollen so as to resemble "hams."

They next erected a fort at Sand Springs, twenty miles from Carson Lake, and another at Cold Springs, thirty-two miles east of Sand Springs. At Cold Springs, Kelley was appointed assistant station-keeper under Jim McNaughton. An outbreak of the Pah-Ute Indians was now in progress, and as the little station was in the midst of the disturbed area, there was plenty of excitement.

One night while Kelley was on guard his attention was attracted by the uneasiness of the horses. Gazing carefully through the dim light, he saw an Indian peering over the outer wall or stockade. The orders of the post were to shoot every Indian that came within range, so Kelley blazed away, but missed his man. In the morning, many tracks were found about the place. This wild shot had probably frightened the prowlers away, saving the station from attack, and certain destruction.

During this same morning, a Mexican pony rider came in, mortally wounded, having been shot by the savages from ambush while passing through a dense thicket in the vicinity known as Quaking Asp Bottom. Although given tender care, the poor fellow died within a few hours after his arrival. The mail was waiting and it must go. Kelley, who was the lightest man in in the place - he weighed but one hundred pounds - was now ordered by the boss to take the dead man's place, and go on with the dispatches. This he did, finishing the run without further incident. On his return trip he had to pass once more through the aspen thicket where his predecessor had received his death wound. This was one of the most dangerous points on the entire trail, for the road zigzagged through a jungle, following a passage-way that was only large enough to admit a horse and rider; for two miles a man could not see more than thirty or forty feet ahead. Kelley was expecting trouble, and went through like a whirlwind, at the same time holding a repeating rifle in readiness should trouble occur. On having cleared the thicket, he drew rein on the top of a hill, and, looking back over his course, saw the bushes moving in a suspicious manner. Knowing there was no live stock in that locality and that wild game rarely abounded there, he sent several shots in the direction of the moving underbrush. The motion soon ceased, and he galloped onward, unharmed.

A few days later, two United States soldiers, while traveling to join their command, were ambushed and murdered in the same thicket.

This was about the time when Major Ormsby's command was massacred by the Utes in the disaster at Pyramid Lake[27], and the Indians everywhere in Nevada were unusually aggressive and dangerous. There were seldom more than three or four men in the little station and it is remarkable that Kelley and his companions were not all killed.

One of Kelley's worst rides, in addition to the episode just related, was the stretch between Cold Springs and Sand Springs for thirty-seven miles without a drop of water along the way.

Once, while dashing past a wagon train of immigrants, a whole fusillade of bullets was fired at Kelley who narrowly escaped with his life. Of course he could not stop the mail to see why he had been shot at, but on his return trip he met the same crowd, and in unprintable language told them what he thought of their lawless and irresponsible conduct. The only satisfaction he could get from them in reply was the repeated assertion, "We thought you was an Indian!"[28] Nor was Kelley the only pony rider who took narrow chances from the guns of excited immigrants. Traveling rapidly and unencumbered, the rider, sunburned and blackened by exposure, must have borne on first glance no little resemblance to an Indian; and especially would the mistake be natural to excited wagon-men who were always in fear of dashing attacks from mounted Indians - attacks in which a single rider would often be deployed to ride past the white men at utmost speed in order to draw their fire. Then when their guns were empty a hidden band of savages would make a furious onslaught. It was the established rule of the West in those days, in case of suspected danger, to shoot first, and make explanations afterward; to do to the other fellow as he would do to you, and do it first!

Added to the perils of the wilderness deserts, blizzards, and wild Indians - the pony riders, then, had at times to beware of their white friends under such circumstances as have been narrated. And that added to the tragical romance of their daily lives. Yet they courted danger and were seldom disappointed, for danger was always near them.

Notes:

[23] Root and Connelley.

[24] Pony riders often alternated "runs" with each other over their respective divisions in the same manner as do railroad train crews at the present time.

[25] "Wild Bill" Hickock was one of the most noted gun fighters that the West ever produced. As marshal of Abilene, Kansas, and other wild frontier towns he be-

came a terror to bad men and compelled them to respect law and order when under his jurisdiction. Probably no man has ever equaled him in the use of the six shooter. Numerous magazine articles describing his career can be found.

[26] Inman & Cody, Salt Lake Trail.

[27] Bancroft.

[28] Indians would sometimes gaze in open-mouthed wonder at the on-rushing ponies. To some of them, the "pony outfit" was "bad medicine" and not to be molested. There was a certain air of mystery about the wonderful system and untiring energy with which the riders followed their course. Unfortunately, a majority of the red men were not always content to watch the Express in simple wonder. They were too frequently bent upon committing deviltry to refrain from doing harm whenever they had a chance.

Chapter VII
Anecdotes of the Trail and Honor Roll

No detailed account of the Pony Express would be complete without mentioning the adventures of Robert Haslam, in those days called "Pony Bob," and William F. Cody, who is known to fame and posterity as "Buffalo Bill."

Haslam's banner performance came about in a matter-of-fact way, as is generally the case with deeds of heroism. On a certain trip during the Ute raids mentioned in the last chapter, he stopped at Reed's Station on the Carson River in Nevada, and found no change of horses, since all the animals had been appropriated by the white men of the vicinity for a campaign against the Indians. Haslam therefore fed the horse he was riding, and after a short rest started for Bucklands[29], the next station which was fifteen miles down the river. He had already ridden seventy-five miles and was due to lay off at the latter place. But on arriving, his successor, a man named Johnson Richardson, was unable or indisposed to go on with the mail[30]. It happened that Division Superintendent W. C. Marley was at Bucklands when Haslam arrived, and, since Richardson would not go on duty, Marley offered "Pony Bob" fifty dollars bonus if he would take up the route. Haslam promptly accepted the proposal, and within ten minutes was off, armed with a revolver and carbine, on his new journey. He at first had a lonesome ride of thirty-five miles to the Sink of the Carson. Reaching the place without mishap, he changed mounts and hurried on for thirty-seven miles over the alkali wastes and through the sand until he came to Cold Springs. Here he again changed horses and once more dashed on, this time for thirty miles without stopping, till Smith's Creek was reached where he was relieved by J. G. Kelley. "Bob" had thus ridden one hundred and eighty-five miles without stopping except to change mounts. At Smith's Creek he slept nine hours and then started back with the return mail. On reaching Cold Springs once more, he found himself in the midst of tragedy. The Indians had been there. The horses had been stolen. All was in ruins. Nearby lay the corpse of the faithful station-keeper. Small cheer for a tired horse and rider! Haslam watered his steed and pounded ahead without rest or refreshment. Before he had covered half the distance to the next station, darkness was falling. The journey was enshrouded with danger. On every side were huge clumps of sage-bush which would offer excellent chances for savages to lie in ambush. The howling of wolves added to the dolefulness of the trip. And haunting him continuously was the thought of the ruined little station and the stiffened corpse behind him. But pony riders were men of courage and nerve, and Bob was no exception. He arrived at Sand Springs safely; but here there was to be no rest nor delay. After reporting the outrage he had just seen, he advised the station man of his danger, and, after changing horses, induced the latter to accompany him on to the Sink of the Carson, which move doubtless saved the latter's life. Reaching the Carson, they found a badly frightened lot of men who had been attacked by the Indians only a few hours previously. A party of fifteen with plenty of arms and ammunition had gathered in the adobe station, which was large enough also to accommodate as, many horses. Nearby was a cool spring of water, and, thus fortified, they were to remain, in a state of siege, if necessary, until the marauders withdrew from that vicinity. Of course they implored Haslam to remain with them and not risk his life venturing away with the mail. But the mail must go; and the schedule, hard as it was, must be maintained. "Bob" had no conception of fear, and so he galloped away, after an hour's rest. And back into Bucklands he came unharmed, after having suffered only three and a half hours of delay. Superintendent Marley, who was still present when the daring rider returned, at once raised his bonus from fifty to one hundred dollars.

Nor was this all of Haslam's great achievement. The west-bound mail would soon arrive, and there was nobody to take his regular run. So after resting an hour and a half, he resumed the saddle and hurried back along his old trail, over the Sierras to Friday's Station. Then "Bob" rested after having ridden three hundred and eighty miles with scarcely eleven hours of lay-off, and within a very few hours of regular schedule time all the way. In speaking of this performance afterwards, Haslam[31] modestly admitted that he was "rather tired," but that "the excitement of the trip had braced him up to stand the journey."

The most widely known of all the pony riders is William F. Cody - usually called "Bill," who in early life resided in Kansas and was raised amid the exciting scenes of frontier life. Cody had an unusually dangerous route between Red Buttes and Three Crossings. The latter place was on the Sweetwater River, and derived its name from the fact that the stream which followed the bed of a rocky cañon, had to be crossed three times within a space of sixty yards. The water coming down from the mountains, was always icy cold and the current swift, deep, and treacherous. The whole bottom of the cañon was often submerged, and in attempting to follow its course along the channel of the stream, both horse and rider were liable to plunge at any time into some abysmal whirlpool. Besides the excitement which the Three Crossings and an Indian country furnished, Cody's trail ran through a region that was often frequented by desperadoes. Furthermore, he had to ford the North Platte at a point where the stream was half a mile in width and in places twelve feet deep. Though the current was at times slow, dangers from quicksand were always to be feared on these prairie rivers. Cody, then but a youth, had to surmount these obstacles and cover his trip at an average of fifteen miles an hour.

Cody entered the Pony Express service just after the line had been organized. At Julesburg he met George Chrisman, an old friend who was head wagon-master for Russell, Majors, and Waddell's freighting department. Chrisman was at the time acting as an agent for the express line, and, out of deference to the youth, he hired him temporarily to ride the division then held by a pony man named Trotter. It was a short route, one of the shortest on the system, aggregating only forty-five miles, and with three relays of horses each way. Cody, who had been accustomed to the saddle all his young life, had no trouble in following the schedule, but after keeping the run several weeks, the lad was relieved by the regular incumbent, and then went east, to Leavenworth, where he fell in with another old friend, Lewis Simpson, then acting as wagon boss and fitting up at Atchison a wagon train of supplies for the old stage line at Fort Laramie and points beyond. Acting through Simpson, Cody obtained a letter of recommendation from Mr. Russell, the head of the firm, addressed to Jack Slade, Superintendent of the division between Julesburg and Rocky Ridge, with headquarters at Horseshoe Station, thirty-six miles west of Fort Laramie, in what is now Wyoming. Armed with this letter, young Cody accompanied Simpson's wagon-train to Laramie, and soon found Superintendent Slade. The superintendent, observing the lad's tender years and frail stature, was skeptical of his ability to serve as a pony rider; but on learning that Cody was the boy who had already given satisfactory service as a substitute some months before, at once engaged him and assigned him to the perilous run of seventy-six miles between Red Buttes and Three Crossings. For some weeks all went well. Then, one day when he reached his terminal at Three Crossings, Cody found that his successor who was to have taken the mail out, had been killed the night before. As there was no extra rider available, it fell to young Cody to fill the dead courier's place until a successor could be procured. The lad was undaunted and anxious for the added responsibility. Within a moment he was off on a fresh horse for Rocky Ridge, eighty-five miles away. Notwithstanding the dangers and great fatigue of the trip, Cody rode safely from Three Crossings to his terminal and returned with the eastbound mail, going back over his own division and into Red Buttes without delay or mishap - an aggregate run of three hundred and twenty-two miles. This was probably the longest continuous performance without formal rest period in the history of this or any other courier service.

Not long afterward, Cody was chased by a band of Sioux Indians while making one of his regular trips. The savages were armed with revolvers, and for a few minutes made it lively for the young messenger. But the superior speed and endurance of his steed soon told; lying flat on the animal's neck, he quickly distanced his assailants and thundered into Sweetwater, the next station, ahead of schedule. Here he found - as so often happened in the history of the express service - that the place had been raided, the keeper slain, and the horses driven off. There was nothing to do but drive his tired pony twelve miles further to Ploutz Station, where he got a fresh horse, briefly reported what he had observed, and completed his run without mishap.

On another occasion[32] it became mysteriously rumored that a certain Pony Express pouch would carry a large sum of currency. Knowing that there was great likelihood of some bandits or "road agents" as they were commonly called getting wind of the consignment and attempting a holdup, Cody hit upon a little emergency ruse. He provided himself with an extra mochila which he stuffed with waste papers and placed over the saddle in the regular position. The pouch containing the currency was hidden under a special saddle blanket. With his customary revolver loaded and ready, Cody then started. His suspicions were soon confirmed, for on reaching a particularly secluded spot, two highwaymen stepped from concealment, and with leveled rifles compelled the boy to stop, at the same time demanding the letter pouch. Holding up his hands as ordered, Cody began to remonstrate with the thugs for robbing the express, at the same time declaring to them that they would hang for their meanness if they carried out their plans. In reply to this they told Cody that they would take their own chances. They knew what he carried and they wanted it. They had no particular desire to harm him, but unless he handed over the pouch without delay they would shoot him full of holes, and take it anyhow. Knowing that to resist meant certain death Cody began slowly to unfasten the dummy pouch, still protesting with much indignation. Finally, after having loosed it, he raised the pouch and hurled it at the head off the nearest outlaw, who dodged, half amused at the young fellow's spirit. Both men were thus taken slightly off their guard, and that instant the rider acted like a flash. Whipping out his revolver, he disabled the farther villain; and before the other, who had stooped to recover the supposed mail sack, could straighten up or use a weapon, Cody dug the spurs into his horse, knocked him down, rode over him and was gone. Before the half-stunned robber could recover himself to shoot, horse and rider were out of range and running like mad for the next station, where they arrived ahead of schedule.

The following is a partial list, so far as is known[33], of the men who rode the Pony Express and contributed to the lasting fame of the enterprise:

Baughn, Melville Beatley, Jim "Boston" Boulton, William Brink, James W. Burnett, John Bucklin, Jimmy Carr, William Carrigan, William Cates, Bill Clark, Jimmy Cliff, Charles Cody, William F. Egan, Major Ellis, J. K. Faust, H. J. Fisher, John Frey, Johnnie Gentry, Jim Gilson, Jim Hamilton, Sam Haslam, Robert Hogan (first name missing) Huntington, Let "Irish Tom" James, William Jenkins, Will D. Kelley, Jay G. Keetley, Jack "Little Yank" Martin, Bob McCall, J. G. McDonald, James McNaughton, Jim Moore, Jim Perkins, Josh Rand, Theodore Richardson, Johnson Riles, Bart Rising, Don C. Roff, Harry Spurr, George Thacher, George Towne, George Wallace, Henry Westcott, Dan Zowgaltz, Jose.

Many of these men were rough and unlettered. Many died deaths of violence. The bones of many lie in unknown graves. Some doubtless lie unburied somewhere in the great West, in the winning of which their lives were lost. Yet be it always remembered, that in the history of the American nation they played an important part. They were bold-hearted citizen knights to whom is due the honors of un-crowned kings.

Notes:

[29] Afterwards named Fort Churchill. This ride took place in the summer of 1860.

[30] Some reports say that Richardson was stricken with fear. That he was probably suffering from overwrought nerves, resulting from excessive risks which his run had involved, is a more correct inference. This is the only case on record of a pony messenger failing to respond to duty, unless killed or disabled.

[31] After the California Pony Express was abandoned, Bob rode for Wells Fargo & Co., between Friday's Station and Virginia City, Nevada, a distance of one hundred miles. He seems to have enjoyed horseback riding, for he made this round-trip journey in twenty-four hours. When the Central Pacific R. R. was built, and this pony line abandoned, Haslam rode for six months a twenty-three mile division between Virginia City and Reno, traveling the distance in less than one hour. To accomplish this feat, he used a relay of fifteen horses. He was afterwards transfered to Idaho where he continued in a similar capacity on a one hundred mile run before quitting the service for a less exciting vocation.

[32] Inman & Cody, Salt Lake Trail.

[33] Root and Connelley's Overland Stage to California.

Chapter VIII
Early Overland Mail Routes

In the history of overland transportation in America, the Pony Express is but one in a series of many enterprises. As emphasized at the beginning of this book, its importance lay in its opportuneness; in the fact that it appeared at the psychological moment, and fitted into the course of events at a critical period, prior to the completion of the telegraph; and when some form of rapid transit between the Missouri River and the Pacific Coast was absolutely needed. To give adequate setting to this story, a brief account of the leading overland routes, of which the Pony Express was but one, seems proper.

Before the middle of the nineteenth century, three great thoroughfares had been established from the Missouri, westward across the continent. These were the Santa Fe, the Salt Lake, and the Oregon trails. All had important branches and lesser stems, and all are today followed by important railroads - a splendid testimonial to the ability of the pioneer pathfinders in selecting the best routes.

Of these trails, that leading to Santa Fe was the oldest, having been fully established before 1824. The Salt Lake and Oregon routes date some twenty years later, coming into existence in the decade between 1840 and 1850. It is incidentally with the Salt Lake trail that the story of the Pony Express mainly deals.

The Mormon settlement of Utah in 1847-48, followed almost immediately by the discovery of gold in California, led to the first mail route[34] across the country, west of the Missouri. This was known as the "Great Salt Lake Mail," and the first contract for transporting it was let July 1, 1850, to Samuel H. Woodson of Independence, Missouri. By terms of this agreement, Woodson was to haul the mail monthly from Independence on the Missouri River to Salt Lake City, twelve hundred miles, and return. Woodson later arranged with some Utah citizens to carry a mail between Salt Lake City and Fort Laramie, the service connecting with the Independence mail at the former place. This supplementary line was put into operation August 1, 1851.

In the early fifties, while the California gold craze was still on, a monthly route was laid out between Sacramento and Salt Lake City[35]. This service was irregular and unreliable; and since the growing population of California demanded a direct overland route, a four year monthly contract was granted to W. F. McGraw, a resident of Maryland. His subsidy from Congress was $13,500.00 a year. In those days it often took a month to get mail from Independence to Salt Lake City, and about six weeks for the entire trip. Although McGraw charged $180.00 fare for each passenger to Salt Lake City, and $300.00 to California, he failed, in 1856. The unexpired contract was then let to the Mormon firm of Kimball & Co., and they kept the route in operation until the Mormon troubles of 1857 when the Government abrogated the agreement.

In the summer of 1857, General Albert Sidney Johnston, later of Civil War fame, was sent out with a Federal army of five thousand men to invade Utah. After a rather fruitless campaign, Johnston wintered at Fort Bridger, in what is southwestern Wyoming, not far from the Utah line. During this interval, army supplies were hauled from Fort Leavenworth with only a few way stations for changing teams. This improvised line, carrying mail occasionally, which went over the old Mormon trail via South Pass, and Forts Kearney, Laramie, and Bridger, was for many months the only service available for this entire region.

The next contract for getting mail into Utah was let in 1858 to John M. Hockaday of Missouri. Johnston's army was then advancing from winter quarters at Bridger toward the valley of Great Salt Lake, and the Government wanted mail oftener then once a month. In consideration of $190,000.00 annually which was to be paid in monthly installments, Hockaday agreed to put on a weekly mail. This route, which ran from St. Joseph to Salt Lake City, was later combined with a line that had been running from Salt Lake to Sacramento, thus making a continuous weekly route to and from California. For the combined route the Government paid $320,000.00 annually. Its actual yearly receipts were $5,142.03.

The discovery of gold in the vicinity of Denver in the summer of 1858 caused another wild excitement and a great rush which led to the establishment in the summer of 1859 of the Leavenworth and Pike's Peak Express, from the Missouri to Denver. As then traveled, this route was six hundred and eighty-seven miles in length. The line as operated by Russell, Majors, and Waddell, and that same year they took over Hockaday's business. As has already been stated, the new firm of Pony Express fame - called the Central Overland California and Pike's Peak Express Co. - consolidated the old California line, which had been run in two sections, East and West, with the Denver line. In addition to the Pony Express it carried on a big passenger and freighting business to and from Denver and California.

Turning now to the lines that were placed in commission farther South. The first overland stage between Santa Fe and Independence was started in May, 1849. This was also a monthly service, and by 1850 it was fully equipped with the famous Concord coaches, which vehicles were soon to be used on every overland route in the West. Within five years, this route, which was eight hundred fifty miles in length and followed the Santa Fe trail, now the route of the Atchison, Topeka, and Santa Fe railroad, had attained great importance. The Government finally awarded it a yearly subsidy of $10,990.00, but as the trail had little or no military protection except at Fort Union, New Mexico, and for hundreds of miles was exposed to the attacks of prairie Indians, the contractors complained because of heavy losses and sought relief of the Post Office and War Departments. Finally they were released from their old contract and granted a new one paying $25,000.00 annually, but even then they fell behind $5,000.00 per year.

By special act passed August 3, 1854, Congress laid out a monthly mail route from Neosho, Missouri, to Albuquerque, New Mexico, with an annual subsidy of $17,000.00. Since the Mexican War this region had come to be of great commercial and military importance. A little later, in March 1855, the route was changed by the Government to run monthly from Independence and Kansas City, Missouri, to Stockton, California, via Albuquerque, and the contractors were awarded a yearly bonus of $80,000.00 This line was also a financial failure.

The early overland routes were granted large subsidies and the privilege of charging high rates for passengers and freight. To the casual observer it may seem strange that practically all these lines operated at a disastrous loss. It should be noted however, that they covered an immense territory, many portions of which were occupied by hostile Indians. It is no easy task to move military forces and supplies thousands of miles through a wilderness. Furthermore, the Indians were elusive and hard to find when sought by a considerable force. They usually managed to attack when and where they were least expected. Consequently, if protection were secured at all, it usually fell to the lot of the stage companies to police their own lines, which was expensive business. Often they waged, single-handed, Indian campaigns of considerable importance, and the frontiersmen whom they could assemble for such duty were sometimes more effective than the soldiers who were unfamiliar with the problems of Indian warfare.

Added to these difficulties were those incident to severe weather, deep snow, and dangerous streams, since regular highways and bridges were almost unknown in the regions traversed. Not to mention the handicap and expense which all these natural obstacles entailed, business on many lines was light, and revenues low.

News from Washington about the creation of the new territory of Utah - in September 1850 - was not received in Salt Lake City until January 1851. The report reached Utah by messenger from California, having come around the continent by way of the Isthmus of Panama. The winters of 1851-52, and 1852-53 were frightfully severe and such expensive delays were not uncommon. The November mail of 1856 was compelled to winter in the mountains.

In the winter of 1856-57 no steady service could be maintained between Salt Lake City and Missouri on account of bad weather. Finally, after a long delay, the postmaster at Salt Lake City contracted with the local firm of Little, Hanks, and Co., to get a special mail to and from Independence. This was accomplished, but the ordeal required seventy-eight days, during which men and animals suffered terribly from cold and hunger. The firm received $1,500.00 for its trouble. The Salt Lake route returned to the Government a yearly income of only $5,000.00.

The route from Independence to Stockton, which cost Uncle Sam $80,000.00 a year, collected in nine months only $1,255.00 in postal revenues, whereupon it was abolished July 1st, 1859.

By the close of 1859 there were at least six different mail routes across the continent from the Missouri to the Pacific Coast. They were costing the Government a total of $2,184,696.00 and returning $339,747.34. The most expensive of these lines was the New York and New Orleans Steamship Company route, which ran semimonthly from New York to San Francisco via Panama. This service cost $738,250.00

annually and brought in $229,979.69. While the steamship people did not have the frontier dangers to confront them, they were operating over a roundabout course, several thousand miles in extent, and the volume of their postal business was simply inadequate to meet the expense of maintaining their business[36].

The steamer schedule was about four weeks in either direction, and the rapidly increasing population of California soon demanded, in the early fifties, a faster and more frequent service. Agitation to that end was thus started, and during the last days of Pierce's administration, in March 1857, the "Overland Mail" bill was passed by Congress and signed by the President. This act provided that the Postmaster-General should advertise for bids until June 30 following: "for the conveyance of the entire letter mail from such point on the Mississippi River as the contractors may select to San Francisco, Cal., for six years, at a cost not exceeding $300,000 per annum for semi-monthly, $450,000 for weekly, or $600,000 for semi-weekly service to be performed semi-monthly, weekly, or semi-weekly at the option of the Postmaster-General." The specifications also stipulated a twenty-five day schedule, good coaches, and four-horse teams.

Bids were opened July 1, 1857. Nine were submitted, and most of them proposed starting from St. Louis, thence going overland in a southwesterly direction usually via Albuquerque. Only one bid proposed the more northerly Central route via Independence, Fort Laramie, and Salt Lake. The Postoffice Department was opposed to this trail, and its attitude had been confirmed by the troubles of winter travel in the past. In fact this route had been a failure for six consecutive winters, due to the deep snows of the high mountains which it crossed.

On July 2, 1857, the Postmaster General announced the acceptance of bid No. "12,587" which stipulated a forked route from St. Louis, Missouri and from Memphis, Tennessee, the lines converging at Little Rock, Arkansas. Thence the course was by way of Preston, Texas; or as nearly as might be found advisable, to the best point in crossing the Rio Grande above El Paso, and not far from Fort Filmore; thence along the new road then being opened and constructed by the Secretary of the Interior to Fort Yuma, California; thence through the best passes and along the best valleys for safe and expeditious staging to San Francisco. On September is following, a six year contract was let for this route. The successful firm at once became known as the "Butterfield Overland Mail Company." Among the firm members were John

Butterfield, Wm. B. Dinsmore, D. N. Barney, Wm. G. Fargo and Hamilton Spencer. The extreme length of the route agreed upon from St. Louis to San Francisco was two thousand seven hundred and twenty-nine miles; the most southern point was six hundred miles south of South Pass on the old Salt Lake route. Because of the out-of-the-way southern course followed, two and one half days more than necessary were nominally-required in making the journey. Yet the postal authorities believed that this would be more than offset by the southerly course being to a great extent free from winter snows.

On September 15, 1858, after elaborate preparations, the overland mails started from San Francisco and St. Louis on the twenty-five day schedule - which was three days less than that of the water route. The postage rate was ten cents for each half ounce; the passenger fare was one hundred dollars in gold. The first trip was made in twenty-four days, and in each of the terminal cities big celebrations were held in honor of the event. And yet today, four splendid lines of railway cover this distance in about three days!

These stages - to use the west-bound route as an illustration - traveled in an elliptical course through Springfield, Missouri, and Fayetteville, Arkansas, to Van Buren, Arkansas, where the Memphis mail was received. Continuing in a south-westerly course, they passed through Indian Territory and the Choctaw Indian reserve - now Oklahoma - crossed the Red River at Calvert's Ferry, then on through Sherman, Fort Chadbourne and Fort Belknap, Texas, through Guadaloupe Pass to El Paso; thence up the Rio Grande River through the Mesilla Valley, and into western New Mexico - now Arizona to Tucson. Then the journey led up the Gila River to Arizona City, across the Mojave desert in Southern California and finally through the San Joaquin Valley to San Francisco.

Today a traveler could cover nearly the same route, leaving St. Louis over the Frisco Railroad, transferring to the Texas Pacific at Fort Worth, and taking the Southern Pacific at El Paso for the remainder of the trip.

As has been shown, the outbreak of the Civil War in the spring of 1861 made it necessary for the Federal Government to transfer this big and important route further north to get it beyond the latitude of the Confederacy. Hence the Southern route was formally abandoned[37] on March 12, 1861, and the equipment removed to the Central or Salt Lake trail where a daily service was inaugurated. About three months was necessary to move all the outfits and in July 1861, the first daily over-land mail - running six times a week - was started between St. Joseph and Placer-ville, California, 1,920 miles by the way of Forts Kearney, Bridger, and Salt Lake City.

The Hannibal and St. Joseph Railroad had been built into St. Joseph and was doing business by February 1859. For some time that city enjoyed the honor of be-ing the eastern stage terminal; but within a year the railroad was extended to Atchi-son, about twenty miles down the stream. The latter place is situated on a bend of the river fourteen miles west of St. Joseph, and so the terminal honors soon passed to Atchison since its westerly location shortened the haul.

In transferring the Butterfield line from the Southern to the Central route, it was merged with the Central Overland California and Pike's Peak Express Company which already included the Leavenworth and Pike's Peak Express Company, under the leadership of General Bela M. Hughes. This line was known to the Government as the Central Overland California Route. As soon as the transfer was completed, through California stages were started on an eighteen day schedule a full week less time than had been required by the Butterfield route, and ten days less than that of the Panama steamers. This was the most famous of all the stage routes, and except for three interruptions, due to Indian outbreaks in 1862, 1864, and 1865, it did busi-ness continuously for several years.

Within a few months came another change of proprietorship, the route passing on a mortgage foreclosure into the hands of Benjamin Holladay, a famous stage line promoter, late in 1861. Early the following year Holladay reorganized the manage-ment under the name of the Overland Stage Line. This seems to have been what today is technically known as a holding company; for until the expiration of the old Butterfield contract in 1863[38], he allowed the business east of Salt Lake City to be carried on by the old C. O. C. & P. P. Co.; west of Salt Lake, the new Overland Line allowed, or sublet the through traffic to a vigorous subsidiary, the Pioneer Stage Line[39].

Holladay was fortunate in securing a new mail contract for the Central route which he now controlled. For supplying a six day letter mail service from the Mis-souri to Placerville together with a way mail to and from Denver and Salt Lake City, he was paid $1,000,000 a year for the three years beginning July 1, 1861. At the expiration of this period he was to get $840,000.

In the meantime gold was discovered in Idaho and Montana, and Holladay, encouraged by his big subsidy from the Government, put stage lines into Virginia City, Montana, and Boise City, Idaho.

In 1866 the Butterfield Overland Despatch, an express and fast freight line, was started above the Smoky Hill route from Topeka and Leavenworth across Kansas to Denver. Within a short time this organization, mainly because of the heavy expense caused by Indian depredations, and was consolidated with the Holladay Company. Just prior to this transfer, Mr. Holladay received from the Colorado Territorial legislature a charter for the "Holladay Overland Mail and Express Company," which was the full and formal name of the new concern. This corporation now owned and controlled stage lines aggregating thirty-three hundred miles. It brought the service up to the highest point of efficiency and used only the best animals and vehicles it was possible to obtain.

In addition to his federal mail bonus, Holladay had the following rates for passenger traffic in force:

In 1863, from Atchison to Denver $75.00

In 1863, from Atchison to Salt Lake City $150.00

In 1863, from Atchison to Placerville $225.00

In 1865, on account of the rise of gold and the depreciation of currency, these rates were increased; the fare from the Missouri River to Denver was changed to $175.00; to Salt Lake $350.00. The California rate varied from $400.00 to $500.00. A year later the fare to Virginia City, Montana, was fixed at $350.00 and the rate to Salt Lake City reduced to $225.00.

These high rates and Indian dangers did not seem to check the desire on the part of the public to make the overland trip. Stages were almost always crowded, and it was usually necessary for one to apply for reservations several days in advance.

Late in the year 1866, Holladay's entire properties[40] were purchased by Wells Fargo and Co. This was a new concern, recently chartered by Colorado, which had been quietly gaining power. Within a short time it had exclusive control of practically all the stage, express, and freighting business in the West and this business it held.

Meanwhile the overland stage and freight lines were rapidly shortening on account of the building of the Pacific railroads, and the terminals of the through routes became merely the temporary ends of the fast growing railway lines. By the early autumn of 1866, the Kansas Pacific had reached Junction City, Kansas, and the Union Pacific was at Fort Kearney, Nebraska. The golden era of the overland stage business was from 1858 to 1866. After that, the old through routes were but fragments "between the tracks" of the Central Pacific and Union Pacific roads which were building East and West toward each other.

Wells Fargo & Co., however, clung to these fragments until the lines met on May 10th, 1869, and a continuous transcontinental railroad was completed. Then they turned their attention to organizing mountain stage and express lines in the railroadless regions of the West, - some of which still exist. And they also turned their energies to the railway express business, in which capacity this great firm, the last of the old stage companies, is now known the world over.

Notes:

[34] Authority for Early Mail Routes is Root and Connelley's Overland Stage to California.

[35] The reader will keep in mind that during the early days of California history, practically all communication between that locality and the East was carried on by steamship from New York via Panama.

[36] In June, 1860, Congress got into trouble with this company over postal compensations. The steamship company, it appears, thought its remuneration too low and it further protested that the diversion of mail traffic, due to the daily Overland Stage Line and the Pony Express would reduce its revenues still further. Congress finally adjourned without effecting a settlement, and the mail, which was far too heavy for the overland facilities to handle at that time, was piling up by the ton awaiting shipment. Matters were getting serious when Cornelius Vanderbilt came to the Government's relief and agreed to furnish steamer service until Congress assembled in March, 1861, provided the Federal authorities would assure him "a fair and adequate compensation." This agreement was effected and the affair settled as agreed. At the expiration of the period, the war and the growing importance of the overland route made steamship service by way of the Isthmus quite obsolete.

[37] The contractors are said to have been awarded $50,000 by the Government for their trouble in haying the agreement broken.

[38] See page 153. Holladay secured possession of the outfits of the C. O. C. & P. P. Exp. Co., between the Missouri and Salt Lake City.

[39] The Pioneer Line which had recently come into power and prominence had gained possession of the equipment west of Salt Lake. This line was owned by Louis and Charles McLane. Louis McLane afterward became President of the Wells Fargo Express Co.

[40] Holladay is said to have received one million five hundred thousand dollars cash, and three hundred thousand dollars in express company stock for his interests. Besides these amounts which covered only the animals, rolling stock, stations, and incidental equipment, Wells Fargo and Co. had to pay full market value for all grain, hay and provisions along the line, amounting to nearly six hundred thousand dollars more.

Chapter IX
Passing of the Pony Express

When Edward Creighton completed the Pacific telegraph, and, on October 24, 1861, began sending messages; by wire from coast to coast, the California Pony Express formally went out of existence. For over three months since July 1, it had been paralleled by the daily overland stage; yet the great efficiency of the semi-weekly pony line in offering quick letter service won and retained its popularity to the very end of its career. And this was in spite of the fact that for several weeks before its discontinuance the pony men had ridden only between the ends of the fast building telegraph which was constructed in two divisions - from the Sierra Nevada Mountains and the Missouri River - at the same time, the lines meeting near the Great Salt Lake.

The people of the far West strongly protested against the elimination of the pony line service. Early in the winter of 1862 it became rumored - perhaps wildly - that the Committee on Finance in the House of Representatives had, for reasons of economy, stricken out the appropriation for the continuance of the daily stage. Whereupon the California legislature[41] addressed a set of joint resolutions to the state's delegation in Congress, imploring not only that the Daily Stage be retained, but that the Pony Express be reestablished. The stage was continued but the pony line was never restored.

As a financial venture the Pony Express failed completely. To be sure, its receipts were sometimes heavy, often aggregating one thousand dollars in a single day. But the expenses, on the other hand, were enormous. Although the line was so great a factor in the California crisis, and in assisting the Federal Government to retain the Pacific Coast, it was the irony of fate that Congress should never give any direct relief or financial assistance to the pony service. So completely was this organization neglected by the government, in so far as extending financial aid was concerned, that its financial failure, as foreseen by Messrs. Waddell and Majors, was certain from the beginning. The War Department did issue army revolvers and cartridges to the riders; and the Federal troops when available, could always be relied upon to protect the line. Yet it was generally left to the initiative and resourcefulness of the company to defend itself as best it could when most seriously menaced by Indians. The apparent apathy regarding this valuable branch of the postal service can of course be partially excused from the fact that the Civil War was in 1861 absorbing all the energies which the Government could summon to its command. And the war, furthermore, was playing havoc with our national finances and piling up a tremendous national debt, which made the extension of pecuniary relief to quasi-private operations of this kind, no matter how useful they were, a remote possibility.

That the stage lines received the assistance they did, under such circumstances, is to be wondered at. Yet it must be borne in mind that at the outset much of the political support necessary to secure appropriations for overland mail routes was derived from southern congressmen who were anxious for routes of communication with the West coast, especially if such routes ran through the Southwest and linked the cotton-growing states with California.

At the very beginning, it cost about one hundred thousand dollars to equip the Pony Express line in those days a very considerable outlay of capital for a private corporation. Besides the purchase of more than four hundred high grade horses, it cost large sums of money to build and equip stations at intervals of every ten or twelve miles throughout the long route. The wages of eighty riders and about four hundred station men, not to mention a score of Division Superintendents was a large item.

Most of the grain used along the line between St. Joseph and Salt Lake City was purchased in Iowa and Missouri and shipped in wagons at a freight rate of from ten cents to twenty cents a pound. Grain and food stuffs for use between Salt Lake City and the Sierras were usually bought in Utah and hauled from two hundred to seven hundred miles to the respective stations. Hay, gathered wherever wild grasses could be found and cured, often had to be freighted hundreds of miles.

The operating expenses of the line aggregated about thirty thousand dollars a month, which would alone have insured a deficit as the monthly income never equaled that amount.

A conspicuous bill of expense which helped to bankrupt the enterprise was for protection against the savages. While this should have been furnished by the Government or the local state or territorial militia, it was the fate of the Company to bear the brunt of one of the worst Indian outbreaks of that decade.

Early in 1860, shortly after the Pony Express was started, the Pah-Utes, mention of whom has already been made, began hostilities under their renowned chieftain Old Winnemucca. The uprising spread; soon the Bannocks and Shoshones espoused the cause of the Utes, and the entire territory of Nevada, Eastern California and Oregon was aflame with Indian revolt. Besides devastating many white settlements wherever they found them, the Indians destroyed nearly every pony station between California and Salt Lake, murdered numbers of employes, and ran off scores of horses. For several weeks the service was paralyzed, and had it been in the hands of faint-hearted men it would have been ended then and there.

The climax came with the defeat and massacre of Major Ormsby's force of about fifty men by the Utes at the battle of Pyramid Lake in western Nevada. Help was finally sent in from a distance, and before the first of June, eight hundred men, including three hundred regulars and a large number of California and Nevada volunteers, had taken the field. This formidable campaign finally served the double purpose of protecting the Pony Express and stage line and in subduing the Indians in a primitive and effective manner. Order was restored and the express service resumed on June 19. Desultory outbreaks, of course, continued to menace the line and all forms of transportation for months afterwards.

During this campaign, the local officers and employes of the express gave valiant service. It was remarkable that they could restore the line so quickly as they did. The total expense of this war to the Company was $75,000, caused by ruined and stolen property and outlays for military supplies incidental to the equipment of volunteers. This onslaught, coming so soon after the enterprise had begun, and when there was already so little encouragement that the line would ever pay out financially, must have disheartened less courageous men than Russell, Majors and Waddell and their associates. It is to their everlasting credit that this group of men possessed the perseverance and patriotic determination to continue the enterprise, even at a certain loss, and in spite of Federal neglect, until the telegraph made it possible to dispense with the fleet pony rider. Not only did they stick bravely to their task of supplying a wonderful mail service to the country, but they even improved their service, increasing it from a weekly to a semi-weekly route, immediately after the disastrous raids of June, 1860. Nor did they hesitate at the instigation of the Government a little later to reduce their postal rates from five dollars to one dollar a half ounce.

This condensed statement shows the approximate deficit which the business incurred:

To equip the line	$100,000
Maintenance at $30,000 per month (for sixteen months)	$480,000
War with the Utes and allied tribes	$75,000
Sundry items	$45,000
Total	$700,000

The receipts are said to have been about $500,000 leaving a debit balance of $200,000. That the Company changed hands in 1861 is not surprising.

While the Pony Express failed in a financial way; it had served the country faithfully and well. It had aided an imperiled Government, helped to tranquilize and retain to the Union a giant commonwealth, and it had shown the practicability of building a transcontinental railroad, and keeping it open for traffic regardless of winter snows. All this Pony Express did and more. It marked the supreme triumph of American spirit, of God-fearing, man-defying American pluck and determination - qualities which have always characterized the winning of the West.

Note:
[41] Senate Documents.

The Codes Of Hammurabi And Moses
W. W. Davies

QTY

The discovery of the Hammurabi Code is one of the greatest achievements of archaeology, and is of paramount interest, not only to the student of the Bible, but also to all those interested in ancient history...

Religion   **ISBN: *1-59462-338-4***   **Pages:132**

MSRP $12.95

The Theory of Moral Sentiments
Adam Smith

QTY

This work from 1749. contains original theories of conscience amd moral judgment and it is the foundation for systemof morals.

Philosophy ISBN: *1-59462-777-0*   **Pages:536**

MSRP $19.95

Jessica's First Prayer
Hesba Stretton

QTY

In a screened and secluded corner of one of the many railway-bridges which span the streets of London there could be seen a few years ago, from five o'clock every morning until half past eight, a tidily set-out coffee-stall, consisting of a trestle and board, upon which stood two large tin cans, with a small fire of charcoal burning under each so as to keep the coffee boiling during the early hours of the morning when the work-people were thronging into the city on their way to their daily toil...

Childrens   ISBN: *1-59462-373-2*

Pages:84

MSRP $9.95

My Life and Work
Henry Ford

QTY

Henry Ford revolutionized the world with his implementation of mass production for the Model T automobile. Gain valuable business insight into his life and work with his own auto-biography... "We have only started on our development of our country we have not as yet, with all our talk of wonderful progress, done more than scratch the surface. The progress has been wonderful enough but..."

Biographies/   ISBN: *1-59462-198-5*

Pages:300

MSRP $21.95

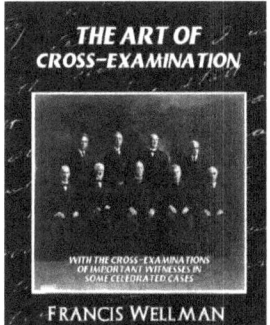

The Art of Cross-Examination
Francis Wellman

QTY

I presume it is the experience of every author, after his first book is published upon an important subject, to be almost overwhelmed with a wealth of ideas and illustrations which could readily have been included in his book, and which to his own mind, at least, seem to make a second edition inevitable. Such certainly was the case with me; and when the first edition had reached its sixth impression in five months, I rejoiced to learn that it seemed to my publishers that the book had met with a sufficiently favorable reception to justify a second and considerably enlarged edition. ..

Reference   **ISBN: *1-59462-647-2***

Pages:412

MSRP $19.95

On the Duty of Civil Disobedience
Henry David Thoreau

QTY

Thoreau wrote his famous essay, On the Duty of Civil Disobedience, as a protest against an unjust but popular war and the immoral but popular institution of slave-owning. He did more than write—he declined to pay his taxes, and was hauled off to gaol in consequence. Who can say how much this refusal of his hastened the end of the war and of slavery ?

Law   **ISBN: *1-59462-747-9***

Pages:48

MSRP $7.45

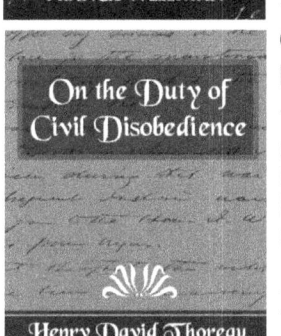

Dream Psychology
Psychoanalysis for Beginners

Sigmund Freud

Dream Psychology Psychoanalysis for Beginners
Sigmund Freud

QTY

Sigmund Freud, born Sigismund Schlomo Freud (May 6, 1856 - September 23, 1939), was a Jewish-Austrian neurologist and psychiatrist who co-founded the psychoanalytic school of psychology. Freud is best known for his theories of the unconscious mind, especially involving the mechanism of repression; his redefinition of sexual desire as mobile and directed towards a wide variety of objects; and his therapeutic techniques, especially his understanding of transference in the therapeutic relationship and the presumed value of dreams as sources of insight into unconscious desires.

Psychology   **ISBN: *1-59462-905-6***

Pages:196

MSRP $15.45

The Miracle of Right Thought
Orison Swett Marden

QTY

Believe with all of your heart that you will do what you were made to do. When the mind has once formed the habit of holding cheerful, happy, prosperous pictures, it will not be easy to form the opposite habit. It does not matter how improbable or how far away this realization may see, or how dark the prospects may be, if we visualize them as best we can, as vividly as possible, hold tenaciously to them and vigorously struggle to attain them, they will gradually become actualized, realized in the life. But a desire, a longing without endeavor, a yearning abandoned or held indifferently will vanish without realization.

Self Help   **ISBN: *1-59462-644-8***

Pages:360

MSRP $25.45

QTY

The Rosicrucian Cosmo-Conception Mystic Christianity *by Max Heindel*   ISBN: *1-59462-188-8*   **$38.95**
The Rosicrucian Cosmo-conception is not dogmatic, neither does it appeal to any other authority than the reason of the student. It is: not controversial, but is: sent forth in the, hope that it may help to clear..   *New Age/Religion Pages 646*

Abandonment To Divine Providence *by Jean-Pierre de Caussade*   ISBN: *1-59462-228-0*   **$25.95**
"The Rev. Jean Pierre de Caussade was one of the most remarkable spiritual writers of the Society of Jesus in France in the 18th Century. His death took place at Toulouse in 1751. His works have gone through many editions and have been republished...   *Inspirational/Religion Pages 400*

Mental Chemistry *by Charles Haanel*   ISBN: *1-59462-192-6*   **$23.95**
Mental Chemistry allows the change of material conditions by combining and appropriately utilizing the power of the mind. Much like applied chemistry creates something new and unique out of careful combinations of chemicals the mastery of mental chemistry...   *New Age Pages 354*

The Letters of Robert Browning and Elizabeth Barret Barrett 1845-1846 vol II   ISBN: *1-59462-193-4*   **$35.95**
by Robert Browning and Elizabeth Barrett   *Biographies Pages 596*

Gleanings In Genesis (volume I) *by Arthur W. Pink*   ISBN: *1-59462-130-6*   **$27.45**
Appropriately has Genesis been termed "the seed plot of the Bible" for in it we have, in germ form, almost all of the great doctrines which are afterwards fully developed in the books of Scripture which follow...   *Religion/Inspirational Pages 420*

The Master Key *by L. W. de Laurence*   ISBN: *1-59462-001-6*   **$30.95**
In no branch of human knowledge has there been a more lively increase of the spirit of research during the past few years than in the study of Psychology, Concentration and Mental Discipline. The requests for authentic lessons in Thought Control, Mental Discipline and...   *New Age/Business Pages 422*

The Lesser Key Of Solomon Goetia *by L. W. de Laurence*   ISBN: *1-59462-092-X*   **$9.95**
This translation of the first book of the "Lernegton" which is now for the first time made accessible to students of Talismanic Magic was done, after careful collation and edition, from numerous Ancient Manuscripts in Hebrew, Latin, and French...   *New Age/Occult Pages 92*

Rubaiyat Of Omar Khayyam *by Edward Fitzgerald*   ISBN:*1-59462-332-5*   **$13.95**
Edward Fitzgerald, whom the world has already learned, in spite of his own efforts to remain within the shadow of anonymity, to look upon as one of the rarest poets of the century, was born at Bredfield, in Suffolk, on the 31st of March, 1809. He was the third son of John Purcell...   *Music Pages 172*

Ancient Law *by Henry Maine*   ISBN: *1-59462-128-4*   **$29.95**
The chief object of the following pages is to indicate some of the earliest ideas of mankind, as they are reflected in Ancient Law, and to point out the relation of those ideas to modern thought.   *Religion/History Pages 452*

Far-Away Stories *by William J. Locke*   ISBN: *1-59462-129-2*   **$19.45**
"Good wine needs no bush, but a collection of mixed vintages does. And this book is just such a collection. Some of the stories I do not want to remain buried for ever in the museum files of dead magazine-numbers an author's not unpardonable vanity..."   *Fiction Pages 272*

Life of David Crockett *by David Crockett*   ISBN: *1-59462-250-7*   **$27.45**
"Colonel David Crockett was one of the most remarkable men of the times in which he lived. Born in humble life, but gifted with a strong will, an indomitable courage, and unremitting perseverance...   *Biographies/New Age Pages 424*

Lip-Reading *by Edward Nitchie*   ISBN: *1-59462-206-X*   **$25.95**
Edward B. Nitchie, founder of the New York School for the Hard of Hearing, now the Nitchie School of Lip-Reading, Inc, wrote "LIP-READING Principles and Practice". The development and perfecting of this meritorious work on lip-reading was an undertaking...   *How-to Pages 400*

A Handbook of Suggestive Therapeutics, Applied Hypnotism, Psychic Science   ISBN: *1-59462-214-0*   **$24.95**
by Henry Munro   *Health/New Age/Health/Self-help Pages 376*

A Doll's House: and Two Other Plays *by Henrik Ibsen*   ISBN: *1-59462-112-8*   **$19.95**
Henrik Ibsen created this classic when in revolutionary 1848 Rome. Introducing some striking concepts in playwriting for the realist genre, this play has been studied the world over.   *Fiction/Classics/Plays 308*

The Light of Asia *by sir Edwin Arnold*   ISBN: *1-59462-204-3*   **$13.95**
In this poetic masterpiece, Edwin Arnold describes the life and teachings of Buddha. The man who was to become known as Buddha to the world was born as Prince Gautama of India but he rejected the worldly riches and abandoned the reigns of power when... Religion/History/Biographies Pages 170

The Complete Works of Guy de Maupassant *by Guy de Maupassant*   ISBN: *1-59462-157-8*   **$16.95**
"For days and days, nights and nights, I had dreamed of that first kiss which was to consecrate our engagement, and I knew not on what spot I should put my lips..."   *Fiction/Classics Pages 240*

The Art of Cross-Examination *by Francis L. Wellman*   ISBN: *1-59462-309-0*   **$26.95**
Written by a renowned trial lawyer, Wellman imparts his experience and uses case studies to explain how to use psychology to extract desired information through questioning.   *How-to/Science/Reference Pages 408*

Answered or Unanswered? *by Louisa Vaughan*   ISBN: *1-59462-248-5*   **$10.95**
Miracles of Faith in China   *Religion Pages 112*

The Edinburgh Lectures on Mental Science (1909) *by Thomas*   ISBN: *1-59462-008-3*   **$11.95**
This book contains the substance of a course of lectures recently given by the writer in the Queen Street Hail, Edinburgh. Its purpose is to indicate the Natural Principles governing the relation between Mental Action and Material Conditions...   *New Age/Psychology Pages 148*

Ayesha *by H. Rider Haggard*   ISBN: *1-59462-301-5*   **$24.95**
Verily and indeed it is the unexpected that happens! Probably if there was one person upon the earth from whom the Editor of this, and of a certain previous history, did not expect to hear again...   *Classics Pages 380*

Ayala's Angel *by Anthony Trollope*   ISBN: *1-59462-352-X*   **$29.95**
The two girls were both pretty, but Lucy who was twenty-one who supposed to be simple and comparatively unattractive, whereas Ayala was credited, as her Bombwhat romantic name might show, with poetic charm and a taste for romance. Ayala when her father died was nineteen...   *Fiction Pages 484*

The American Commonwealth *by James Bryce*   ISBN: *1-59462-286-8*   **$34.45**
An interpretation of American democratic political theory. It examines political mechanics and society from the perspective of Scotsman James Bryce   *Politics Pages 572*

Stories of the Pilgrims *by Margaret P. Pumphrey*   ISBN: *1-59462-116-0*   **$17.95**
This book explores pilgrims religious oppression in England as well as their escape to Holland and eventual crossing to America on the Mayflower, and their early days in New England...   *History Pages 268*

QTY

The Fasting Cure *by Sinclair Upton*　　　　　　　　ISBN: *1-59462-222-1*　**$13.95**
In the Cosmopolitan Magazine for May, 1910, and in the Contemporary Review (London) for April, 1910, I published an article dealing with my experi-
ences in fasting. I have written a great many magazine articles, but never one which attracted so much attention... New Age/Self Help/Health Pages 164

Hebrew Astrology *by Sepharial*　　　　　　　　　ISBN: *1-59462-308-2*　**$13.45**
In these days of advanced thinking it is a matter of common observation that we have left many of the old landmarks behind and that we are now pressing
forward to greater heights and to a wider horizon than that which represented the mind-content of our progenitors... Astrology Pages 144

Thought Vibration or The Law of Attraction in the Thought World　　ISBN: *1-59462-127-6*　**$12.95**

by William Walker Atkinson　　　　　　　　　　　　Psychology/Religion Pages 144

Optimism *by Helen Keller*　　　　　　　　　　　ISBN: *1-59462-108-X*　**$15.95**
Helen Keller was blind, deaf, and mute since 19 months old, yet famously learned how to overcome these handicaps, communicate with the world, and
spread her lectures promoting optimism. An inspiring read for everyone... Biographies/Inspirational Pages 84

Sara Crewe *by Frances Burnett*　　　　　　　　　ISBN: *1-59462-360-0*　**$9.45**
In the first place, Miss Minchin lived in London. Her home was a large, dull, tall one, in a large, dull square, where all the houses were alike, and all the
sparrows were alike, and where all the door-knockers made the same heavy sound... Childrens/Classic Pages 88

The Autobiography of Benjamin Franklin *by Benjamin Franklin*　　ISBN: *1-59462-135-7*　**$24.95**
The Autobiography of Benjamin Franklin has probably been more extensively read than any other American historical work, and no other book of its kind
has had such ups and downs of fortune. Franklin lived for many years in England, where he was agent... Biographies History Pages 332

Name	
Email	
Telephone	
Address	
City, State ZIP	

☐ **Credit Card**　　　　☐ **Check / Money Order**

Credit Card Number	
Expiration Date	
Signature	

Please Mail to:　Book Jungle
　　　　　　　　　PO Box 2226
　　　　　　　　　Champaign, IL 61825
or Fax to:　　　630-214-0564

ORDERING INFORMATION

web: *www.bookjungle.com*
email: *sales@bookjungle.com*
fax: *630-214-0564*
mail: *Book Jungle PO Box 2226 Champaign, IL 61825*
or PayPal *to sales@bookjungle.com*

Please contact us for bulk discounts

DIRECT-ORDER TERMS

**20% Discount if You Order
Two or More Books**
Free Domestic Shipping!
Accepted: Master Card, Visa,
Discover, American Express